The Slave of the Thieves' Market

By G. H. Teed

Illustrated by Val Reading

First published in the Union Jack magazine,
New Series, No. 1026, 9 June 1923.

Stillwoods Edition

Stillwoods.Blogspot.Ca

Catalogue Information:
Title: The Slave of the Thieves' Market
Author: G. H. Teed (1886-1938)
Illustrated by: Val Reading
First published anonymously in the Union Jack magazine, New
    Series, No. 1026, 9 June 1923.
This Edition: Stillwoods 2023
ISBN Canada: 978-1-998819-11-9
Blog: Stillwoods.Blogspot.Ca
Author Blog: http://ghteed.blogspot.com/
Storefront: http://www.lulu.com/spotlight/lulubook22

https://tinyurl.com/ve25d42s This link should go to a spreadsheet of all known Teed stories. The list is annotated with various information on the stories and my progress with recapturing the work. The library of Teed's stories increases almost weekly. Check at the Lulu.Com for the latest arrivals. Search for Teed. /drf

Keywords: Sexton Blake, Wu Ling, San Francisco, Canton

Cautionary Note: This series of books by Stillwoods are intended to make the stories of G. H. Teed, born in New Brunswick, Canada, available to collectors and researchers. The editor, or rather digitizer has not altered the original publication.

This story may contain language and racial terms that are not appropriate to today. I apologize for them; I know that the author was using his voice to excite and entertain an adventurous English audience. These works were published from 82 to 110 years ago. Most every work has characters of redeeming ethnicity within.

I hope you enjoy and share these stories; I have.

Doug Frizzle

Contains some racial language

A long, complete story of SEXTON BLAKE and TINKER in San Francisco and Canton. This breezy yarn introduces also Sir GORDON SADDLER and WU LING, the Chief of the dread Brotherhood of the Yellow Beetle. It records another thrilling episode in the battle for the sacred Ling-tse vase. As a typical U. J. story, is well up to sample.

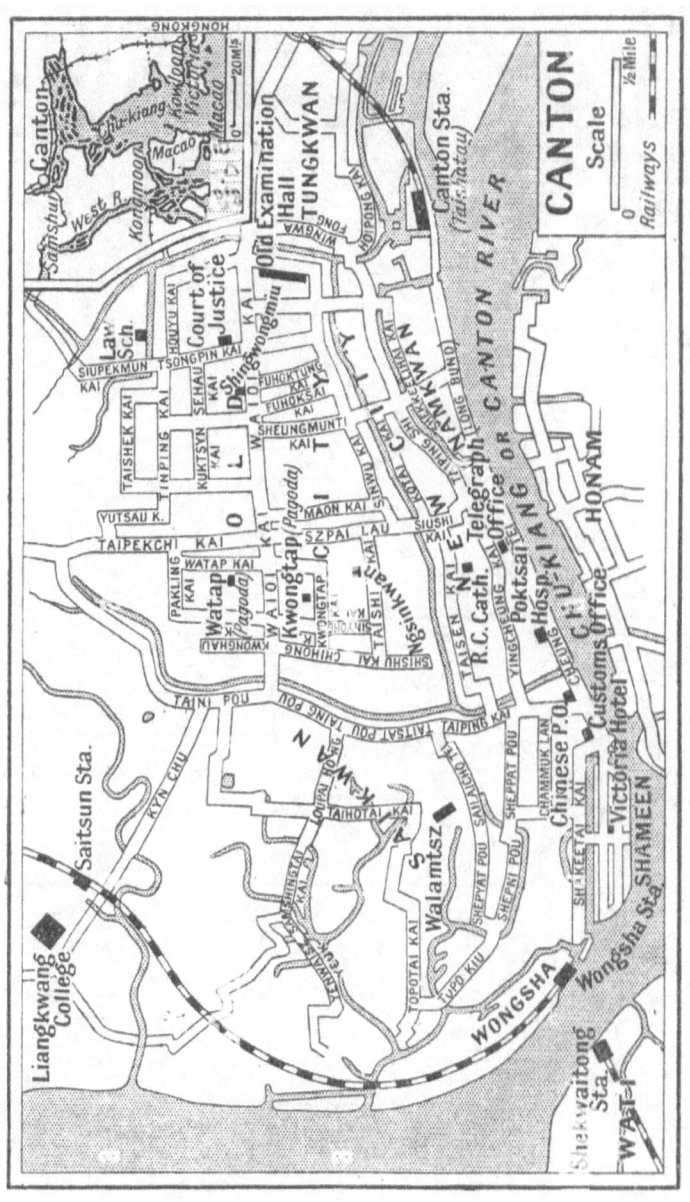

The SLAVE of the THIEVES' MARKET

A long, complete story of SEXTON BLAKE and TINKER in San Francisco and Canton. This breezy yarn introduces also Sir GORDON SADDLER and WU LING, the Chief of the dread Brotherhood of the Yellow Beetle. It records another thrilling episode in the battle for the sacred Ling-tse vase. As a typical U.J. story, is well up to sample.

[THE FIRST CHAPTER.]

A Tarpon—A Battle For Life—And a Coincidence.

"YOU'VE got him, guv'nor—you've got him! Oh, my sainted aunt! He must be the grand-daddy of them all. Let him have it, guv'nor! He'll take a mile at this rate. Wow! He nearly had us over then. He's gone deep—now he's off again. Oh. Oh! Hold him, guv'nor! Wow!"

"Keep steady there, Tinker! Between the pair of you we will be over. Stay where you are. No, don't bother about the gaff—this fellow will fight for an hour yet. There he goes again. He'll take all the line at this rate. Steady there, you crazy ass!"

Sexton Blake was half kneeling, half standing in the bottom of a sturdily-built, canoe-shaped craft, braking down gently on his reel, while the heavy silk line flew out as if some wizard of speed and rage was at that other end of it.

Tinker was in the bow, standing in a bent position, his hands resting each on a gunwale, the while he watched the course of the line. He was wildly excited, and was venting his feelings in a running comment of yells and jerky phrases.

And well he might be excited; for there could be no doubt that Blake had struck a really king pin tarpon—the biggest, strongest, fighting fish that can be landed by the line.

And a few seconds later, as Blake seized his opportunity to reel in some of the slackening line, Tinker's anticipations were more than fulfilled, for up from the blue surface of the Gulf of California there flashed a marvel of silver-spangled grandeur—an almost unbelievably graceful monster for one of such enormous bulk. A veritable monarch of the ocean—a magnificent specimen of the fighting silver king tarpon—fully seven feet from tip to tip, and bulking to more than two hundred pounds.

Even the ordinarily composed Blake was moved to an exclamation of amazement as the silver giant flashed above the water, then went down in a fountain of multi-coloured spray as the ocean surface was shattered by the terrific impact.

Then he was off again, and as the line tautened the canoe began to move along as Sexton Blake, frowning under the strain, and with the sinews in his wrist standing out like steel wire, braked down on the reel with infinite care, keeping the strain just clear of the snapping-point. It seemed incredible that the giant silver king could long be held by that fragile-looking rod, and the seemingly futile bit of silk that was quivering like a live thing as the tarpon raced at express speed deep down in the blue depths.

But there was a master hand holding that rod—a hand which yielded or tautened to every slightest vibration which reached it ; which sensed the tearing, raging convulsions of the giant as truly as the hand of a master horseman might sense the mouth of his mount.

Off to the right, about a quarter of a mile distant, a low, rakish motor-boat lay idly rocking on the face of the gulf. Nearer at hand were two other canoes also containing fishermen. The occupants of them were now standing watching in breathless interest, while Sexton Blake, the guest of Colonel Bob Fairfax, the owner of the boat, and also of the great white villa which could be seen on the shore, fought his fight with the biggest silver king any of them had ever seen.

Further away were other canoes, and, at a still greater distance, motor boats, schooners, and other craft of every conceivable form and size. For in the season the Gulf of California is the resort of sportsmen, and those who fish for commercial reasons, on a tremendous scale.

It became very soon evident to Blake and Tinker, as well as to those others who watched, that the battle between man and sea monarch was going to be no ordinary affair. As the tarpon forged ahead at express speed the steady pressure which Blake was keeping upon the reel brake allowed the canoe to gather more and more speed, until it was racing through the water as if propelled by some submarine force, as indeed it was.

THE FIRST CHAPTER.   *A Tarpon —A Battle For Life —And a Coincidence.*

"YOU'VE got him, guv'nor —you've got him! Oh, my sainted aunt! He must be the grand-daddy of them all. Let him have it, guv'nor! He'll take a mile at this rate. Wow! He nearly had us over then. He's gone deep —now he's off again. Oh. Oh! Hold him, guv'nor! Wow!"

"Keep steady there, Tinker! Between the pair of you we will be over. Stay where you are. No, don't bother about the gaff —this fellow will fight for an hour yet. There he goes again. He'll take all the line at this rate. Steady there, you crazy ass!"

Sexton Blake was half kneeling, half standing in the bottom of a sturdily-built, canoe-shaped craft, braking down gently on his reel, while the heavy silk line flew out as if some wizard of speed and rage was at that other end of it.

Tinker was in the bow, standing in a bent position, his hands resting each on a gunwale, the while he watched the course of the line. He was wildly excited, and was venting his feelings in a running comment of yells and jerky phrases.

And well he might be excited; for there could be no doubt that Blake had struck a really king pin tarpon —the biggest, strongest, fighting fish that can be landed by the line.

And a few seconds later, as Blake seized his opportunity to reel in some of the slackening line, Tinker's anticipations were more than fulfilled, for up from the blue surface of the Gulf of California there flashed a marvel of silver-spangled grandeur —an almost unbelievably graceful monster for one of such enormous bulk. A veritable monarch of the ocean —a magnificent specimen of the fighting silver king tarpon —fully seven feet from tip to tip, and bulking to more than two hundred pounds.

Even the ordinarily composed Blake was moved to an exclamation of amazement as the silver giant flashed above the water, then went down in a fountain of multi-coloured spray as the ocean surface was shattered by the terrific impact.

Then he was off again, and as the line tautened the canoe began to move along as Sexton Blake, frowning under the strain, and with the sinews in his wrist standing out like steel wire, braked down on the reel with infinite care, keeping the strain just clear of the snapping-point. It seemed incredible that the giant silver king could long be held by that fragile-looking rod, and the seemingly futile bit of silk that was quivering like a live thing as the tarpon raced at express speed deep down in the blue depths.

But there was a master hand holding that rod —a hand which yielded or tautened to every slightest vibration which reached it; which sensed the tearing, raging convulsions of the giant as truly as the hand of a master horseman might sense the mouth of his mount.

Off to the right, about a quarter of a mile distant, a low, rakish motor-boat lay idly rocking on the face of the gulf. Nearer at hand were two other canoes also containing fishermen. The occupants of them were now standing watching in breathless interest, while Sexton Blake, the guest of Colonel Bob Fairfax, the owner of the boat, and also of the great white villa which could be seen on the shore, fought his fight with the biggest silver king any of them had ever seen.

Farther away were other canoes, and, at a still greater distance, motor boats, schooners, and other craft of every conceivable form and size. For in the season the Gulf of California is the resort of sportsmen, and those who fish for commercial reasons, on a tremendous scale.

It became very soon evident to Blake and Tinker, as well as to those others who watched, that the battle between man and sea monarch was going to be no ordinary affair. As the tarpon forged ahead at express speed the steady pressure which Blake was keeping upon the reel brake allowed the canoe to gather more and more speed, until it was racing through the water as if propelled by some submarine force, as indeed it was.

Tinker had now grasped a paddle, and, at imminent risk of capsizing the craft, had managed to reach the stern, where he thrust the paddle in and did his best to guide the canoe in the wake of the tarpon.

He realised only too well what would happen if he failed to do so, for a sudden jerk on the line, which Blake was "feeling" to the Nth degree of tension, would cause it to snap. But between them they kept the direction, and at every opportunity Blake reeled in as much of the slack as he dared.

For a full half-hour the terrific struggle went on. So far the tarpon seemed as vigorous as ever, while his would-be conqueror was dripping sweat under the strain of the terrific effort of hand and brain

2

which he was making.

What line he managed to reel in was whipped out again almost at once. Again and again was this repeated, and at the end of the first half-hour the tarpon made one magnificent dash, greater than any since Blake had struck, which carried the line perilously close to its end. But by skilful manoeuvring Tinker saved the situation, and as the tarpon dashed off on to a new course Blake managed to reel in again.

Thus it went until a full hour had passed, and it was not until then that Blake felt a surge of exultation sweep through him as he realised the silver king was tiring.

Less frequent now were the wild dashes; greater and greater were the lengths which Blake was able to reel in; surer and surer did he feel that the tarpon was being brought to defeat. But that did not mean an early victory, as he very soon discovered, for after a few minutes of seeming inertia the king began his fight all over again.

At first it felt to Blake as if he possessed all that terrific speed and strength which he had possessed an hour before. But at the end of a quarter of an hour the rushes again began to grew less frequent, the opportunities of reeling in increased, the canoe was now moving slowly over the water, while the tarpon was apparently sulking in the blue depths.

But flash after flash of rage he showed, and twice he threw himself high out of the water, a perfectly regal thing of grace and beauty, to fall submerged in the gleaming facets of the shimmering fountain his upheaval had caused.

Then, however, the cool brain behind that wrist of steel began to direct the final manoeuvres in the battle royal.

Tinker was breathless while he watched. He was confident now that Blake would win, but so tensely was he sympathising with his master, that it was as if he was the one preparing to "count coup." Nearer and nearer the great fighter was brought until time and again his silvery armour flashed close to the sun-beaten surface.

Then, at a sign from Blake, Tinker eased his paddle inboard and crept forward to where the gaff lay. Holding it ready, he stood waiting until, in one final manoeuvre, Blake had brought the tarpon in close.

For the space of three seconds the line grew taut as if the monster would make one final dash for freedom; but then, in a truly masterly manipulation of the rod, Blake brought his splendid prize alongside. Swiftly Tinker struck the long barb of the gaff, biting deep into the silvery armour.

There was a sudden convulsion. For a few moments it seemed as if the thrashing giant would overturn the canoe in its death throes. Then he rolled over, and, under the gentle persuasion of Blake's line, came in helplessly to the side. The battle was over, and as Blake and Tinker gazed down at the royal king of the deep, they knew that it was almost, if not quite, a record-breaker.

They were recalled to their surroundings by a perfect pandemonium of noise which broke out behind them. Glancing up, they saw that the motor-launch had picked up the other canoes, and was towing them in line towards the scene of the victory. It was only then that Blake and Tinker realised how far the frantic dashes of the tarpon must have carried them. As a matter of fact, they had been drawn more than two miles from where the motor-launch had lain, although they did not know the exact distance until later.

Now the siren of the launch was being blown like a thing demented. All hands in the canoes were filling the air with a mixture of Indian and college yells. It was their exuberant tribute to the victory of the British guest, and they intended to do full justice to it, for that first flash of the king had told them that Blake was pitted against a real champion.

In a welter of howling enthusiasm Blake and Tinker were hauled aboard the launch, while the other canoes pulled in, and their occupants tumbled over the side. Then, in a silence which was in sharp contrast to the previous pandemonium, the great silver king was hauled up and laid along the deck. Nor was the silence broken then.

Every man, a true fisherman and a true sportsman, stood in silent tribute to the fallen monarch. It was Colonel Bob Fairfax who first broke the silence.

"Blake, old man," he said, with feeling, "I'll wager anything anyone wants to name that you have landed a record-breaker! He's a beauty. We must get him ashore and weigh and measure him."

"I'd rather land a silver king like that than a dozen tunas at the full weight." broke in a rugged old gentleman, who had fished every ocean on the globe. "I'll not say he is the biggest ever caught, but he won't be ashamed in the comparison. Mr. Blake, sir, you have my heartiest congratulations."

"There is more fight in one silver king than half a dozen tunas!" remarked the colonel "The biggest silver king I ever saw was one landed off the Silver King Tarpon Club, in Florida. It is in the club trophy-room now, and I'll wager this fellow will run him close. We must take his weight and measurements at once."[1]

Standing over the fallen giant, they drifted into reminiscence after reminiscence, while the motor-launch raced for the shore. As they touched at the little jetty, which had been built at the water's edge of Colonel Fairfax's property, they all tumbled out. The colonel gave instructions to three of his Mex peons to carry the tarpon up to the house, and, escorted by a bodyguard of veteran sportsmen, the procession started.

The villa was a building after the California type of bungalow — a wide, roomy, stone-built, residence, fitted like a club sporting lodge, and possessing every appurtenance that a wealthy sportsman could install. It was surrounded by cool trees, and about the place could be seen a dozen or more Chinese "boys," clad in spotless white, and thoroughly efficient; Colonel Bob was a fine gentleman and a fine sportsman, and nothing gave him greater happiness than to have his house filled with kindred souls.

It was by sheer accident he had run into Sexton Blake and Tinker in San Diego. The famous criminologist and his assistant had been on the point of going north to San Francisco before crossing the continent to sail for England after a disappointing journey down through California in pursuit of Blake's ancient enemy, Prince Wu Ling, sinister foe of the races of the West, and supreme head of that powerful organisation known as the Brotherhood of the Yellow Beetle. And, what was of far more account to Sexton Blake and his old friend, Sir Gordon Saddler, the mystery man of 'Frisco, Wu Ling was the present possessor of that symbol of supreme, political power in China, the ancient and sacred Ling-tse vase.

---

[1] The giant tuna, which is to be found in the Gulf of California and off the Pacific coast of California, runs individually up to four hundred pounds. The tuna is a magnificent fish, and it is no easy matter to land one. But there isn't a harder fighter in the sea than the regal silver king, which visits the waters of the Gulf of California very seldom. He is as swift as the deadly barracuda and as implacable as the killer-whale. He is found most plentifully in southern waters, and the largest on record have been taken off the coast of Florida. Therefore, apart from the fact, that Blake had landed one pretty close to a record-breaker, his feat is doubly worthy of record from the fact that he landed it in waters where the silver king is a rare visitor.

Those who have read the record of that case will recall how, when Sir Gordon thought the vase was safe in his custody, owing to the fact that it was protected by the sacred hair of Confucius —a taboo which he knew Wu Ling would never dare to break —the taboo had been broken by the command of the prince.[2]

It had meant the utter annihilation of one of the inner council of the Brotherhood; but such was the power Wu Ling wielded, the chosen one never faltered in his deed, though believing that the breaking of the taboo meant eternal darkness for his soul.

It was a daring stroke, and one which only a person of Wu Ling's calibre would have dared. But for the time it had succeeded, and then, after a mad chase down through the state —after parting at San Diego, where Blake took up one part of the pursuit by a converted T.B.D.[3], while Tinker continued on by car —at the very moment when it looked as if Wu Ling was at last in their grasp, some accident had occurred on the ship on which the prince was escaping. The explosion was terrific, and had occurred just as Tinker had taken his great plunge for life from the spanker gaff.

What had become of Wu Ling or the Ling-tse vase neither Blake nor Tinker knew. About them had been many other craft, and among those scores of bobbing heads in the dusk it had been impossible to pick out one which might be that of Wu Ling. He may have been killed by the explosion. He may have been drowned; he may have been saved.

It was impossible to discover a single definite clue. So, perforce, Blake had given up the chase, and, labouring under an acute sense of disappointment, had started back for 'Frisco.

If he had only known that Wu Ling was dead he wouldn't have cared two straws about the Ling-tse vase. But who could tell when that sinister figure might, appear again? He had overcome such stupendous obstacles in the past that Sexton Blake was not prepared to believe that he was dead until he should gaze with his own eyes upon the stiffened features.

---

[2] The Tabu of Confucius, UNION JACK · New series · Issue 1,023 · 19/5/1923, /drf

[3] Although the term "destroyer" had been used interchangeably with "TBD" and "torpedo boat destroyer" by navies since 1892, the term "torpedo boat destroyer" had been generally shortened to simply "destroyer" by nearly all navies by the First World War. /drf, wiki

In this mood it is not strange that Blake should have been only too glad to join Colonel Fairfax's house-party, and to try and forget, in the chase after the lordly tuna and the kingly tarpon, all that had gone before.

And as those exuberant men, more like a bunch of schoolboys than staid and powerful business magnates, professional men, and financiers, crowded round the tarpon, while the Mex peons hoisted him up to the triangle weighing beam, and while a white-jacketed Chinese "boy" stood ready with shining blade to make the first cut along that silvery surface as soon as the weight and measurements were checked, Blake smiled in genuine pleasure.

"Two fifty —two fifty-one —two fifty-two and seven ounces!" intoned the voice of the colonel, rising at the last word to a shout of triumph. "They'll never smash that record on this coast, Blake! That means a special celebration to-night! Thank Heaven we are over the border in Mexico, and that I have some real vintage in the cellar!

"Now, then, Dicky" —this to one of the younger men— "get your camera and photograph his majesty before Chan cuts him!"

Another delay while the one called Dicky ran off, to return a few moments later with a large kodak. Then the ceremony of photographing Blake and Tinker, one on each side of the silver king, with Blake holding his rod while Tinker grasped the gaff, was concluded. That done, the colonel raised his hand in signal to Chan, the Chinese boy, and, as the point of the blade sank into the silver skin, most of the crowd turned away to seek a cool drink in the front porch.

But not so Blake and Tinker, nor their host. All three stood close by while the capable Chinese boy slit the giant body from end to end. Then they waited while he opened up the inside; but as the blade opened the great stomach, only Sexton Blake caught a momently glimpse of something of a bluish tinge which roused his curiosity.

He stepped forward and bent his head, and, as if to give him room to see better, Chan, the Chinese boy, moved back a little. Blake peered into the gaping orifice, but there was nothing to be seen but just the mutilated stomach of the fish.

And yet it was curious. He could have sworn that he had glimpsed some alien matter as the Chinese boy had opened the taut sac. What it was he had not an idea, except that there had been a vague chord struck in his memory. It could not be that his eyes had tricked him. He had seen it all right. But why was it not there now?

He turned and shot a swift glance at Chan. The Celestial was standing humbly enough, as if waiting for Blake to complete his examination. Blake noted that both hands were hanging loosely by his side. His gaze returned to the tarpon, and it was then, in that second instant of first contact, a terrific thought burst upon him.

He said nothing. He drew aside, regardless of the fact that both Colonel Fairfax and Tinker were looking at him curiously. He took out his cigarette-case and lit a cigarette. For a few moments longer he watched the Celestial, who had now returned to his work. Then he drawled:

"Well, I think I have had enough of this. It was pretty warm work. I think it would be a good idea to follow the example of the others."

Both his host and Tinker agreed. So, after a few further words of instruction to Chan, the colonel led the way towards the front of the house. But no sooner had they turned the corner than Blake grasped the colonel by the arm.

"Must have a quiet word with you at once, colonel," he said curtly. "It's important and urgent."

Accustomed to many an odd situation, the colonel betrayed no surprise at Blake's words.

"In here," he said in even tones; and, with that, he drew Blake through a side path along to a space some distance away, which was soon revealed as a wide swimming-pool.

Tinker followed, and, as Blake drew up behind a giant hedge, the lad listened in dumbfounded amazement while his master gave the colonel a description, accompanied by apparently irrelevant detail, of the affair that had brought them down through Southern California and across the Mexican border. But the lad got a greater shock when, as he finished, Blake said:

"And I am willing to wager any odds that I have seen that sacred Ling-tse vase within the last ten minutes, colonel."

"But where, Blake —but where?" asked the bewildered colonel. "If it is anywhere here on my property, you have only to point it out, and it is yours."

"It is on your property," answered Blake. "Listen. When your Chinese boy was cutting open the stomach of the tarpon I glimpsed something inside. At first I didn't grasp what it could be, except that it

8

was an object of some sort alien to the natural diet of the tarpon. It was not food, either undigested, or partially digested. It was a hard object which had gone accidentally through the maw of that fish.

"And now I know it was nothing less titan the Ling-tse vase! We can never tell exactly how it found its way into the stomach of the tarpon, but it is a reasonable supposition that when Wu Ling was hurled into the sea by the explosion the vase was torn free from his possession, and as it sank through the clear water the colour of it may have attracted the vagrant notice of the very tarpon I hooked to-day.

"However that may have been, it found its way through the tarpon's maw, and I am equally certain that your Chinese boy spotted it as soon as I did."

"Then what became of it?" asked the bewildered colonel.

"The boy palmed it and slipped it inside his jacket. It disappeared as if by magic. I could not accuse him before you, because he is your servant. But I shall be very grateful if you will have him searched before he has an opportunity to hide it."

"You bet your life I will!" exclaimed the colonel. "Come on! We will go through him now!"

He led the way at a run back towards where they had left Chan working on the tarpon. The giant still hung from the great beam. The knife was sticking into the silver armour. But of Chan there was no sign. He had faded away as silently as an elusive shadow. And although they raced at once towards the servants' quarters, Sexton Blake had a feeling that the Celestial was gone for good.

And Blake was right.

THE search of the servants' quarters, and afterwards of the whole estate, was purely a perfunctory matter.

Blake had not the faintest hope that Chan would be found. Therefore he was not disappointed when the search failed. The other Chinese boys simply chorused "No savvy!" in reply to the colonel's questions, and he, like Blake, knew that it was useless to press them further. The numerous Mex peons about the place either could not tell anything or were too much in fear of the Chinese to give any information.

So the result was that the better part of an hour was lost, while Chan was just that much to the good.

It was impossible to try to guess which way he would make. He might take to the mesquite and chapparal, and work his way across Mexico to the eastern seaboard; he might make straight for the gulf and escape by one of the numerous Chinese fishing-craft there; or he might cross the border into the United States and try to reach 'Frisco.

In any event, Blake felt certain that Chan was but an agent for some power much higher up, and that, on accidentally discovering the sacred Ling-tse vase, he had acted almost automatically. Not a Celestial but would know that vase when he saw it, and, no matter how completely astounded he might be at coming upon it under such dramatic circumstances, his Oriental subtlety would rise to the occasion —as, indeed, Chan's had.

In fact, he had beaten Blake by the veriest fraction of a second. But that fractional space of time had been sufficient for his purpose, and Blake was more than a little chagrined when he reflected how nearly he had had the vase in his possession.

If he had but shot out his hand at the first instant of seeing it! If he had not allowed his amazement to hold him motionless for that infinitesimal space of time!

But self-reproach served him not at all now. Chan had acted one flash sooner, with the result that the wily Celestial was now legging it Heaven alone knew where.

Blake opined, if he only knew the whereabouts of Wu Ling, he might be able, even then, to outwit Chan, for he was taking it for granted that Chan was a member of the Brotherhood of the Yellow Beetle. But in that Blake was wrong, as he was to find out in the very near future. He hadn't an idea what had become of Wu Ling after the explosion of the five-master; and he would have been still more puzzled if he had guessed for a single instant that did Wu Ling but know how the vase had been found, and how it had been spirited away, he would have been even more perturbed than was Blake.

It was a queer game upon which Blake had embarked, and he was to find that it was to develop into a much more complicated battle of wits before he was finished with it.

He had bound Colonel Fairfax to silence, and knew, of course, that the secret was perfectly safe with him. Whatever the colonel had felt at the disclosure, he had said nothing, nor did he attempt to question Blake further, it was sufficient for him to know that the mysterious vase, which had evidently been swallowed by the giant silver king tarpon, was an object of intense interest to his friend, and that one of his own Chinese boys had made off with it.

He had half-a-dozen suggestions to make, but Blake firmly vetoed them all.

"You are extremely kind, colonel," he said smilingly, "but I really cannot permit you to discommode yourself further. If we had anything definite to go on, I should say yes. But to look for the 'boy' now would be like trying to pick that particular tarpon out of the waters of the gulf, and such a thing doesn't happen but once in a lifetime.

"It is almost uncanny that this vase —the only remaining one of the pair —should have been preserved in such a manner. It is almost as if the ancient gods of the past were determined to guard it. And before I see it again, if ever, the chase will be a long one."

"It reminds me of the whale and Jonah," remarked the colonel, with a laugh. "What do you say, Tinker?"

"Well, sir, I agree with you," responded the lad. "I'll bet, if a fish can suffer from indigestion, that tarpon had a good attack of it."

They changed the subject of conversation as they approached the front porch where the rest of the guests were gathered, sipping long, cool drinks, and as the trio mounted the steps none of the others guessed what had taken place during the past quarter of an hour. Nor were they enlightened. But as Blake seated himself, a Chinese houseboy approached with a small silver tray, on which reposed a telegram.

Wondering somewhat whom it was from, Blake, with a word of

apology, took it and tore it open. And as he read the contents he knew that his next move had been decided for him, for it was from Sir Gordon Saddler, the mystery man of 'Frisco, and ran as follows:

"Very important news. Can you come on to 'Frisco at once. Have located our man. —S."

Which, of course, meant to Blake that, through his vast network of spies, Sir Gordon had, in some way, managed to discover the whereabouts of Wu Ling. As soon as he had an opportunity, he informed Colonel Bob that it would be necessary for him and Tinker to leave that same evening, and, although his host begged him to put off his departure until the morrow, Blake courteously stuck to his point. He was naturally sorry to miss the banquet which had been planned in honour of his great capture, but it couldn't be helped. So the colonel placed one of his cars at their disposal, and in the late afternoon they started for San Diego, across the border.

On the way they discussed in low tones (the driver was an American, but, nevertheless, they were taking no chances of being overheard) the subject-matter of the telegram.

"If the 'boy,' Chan is making for Wu Ling, then, if we get a telegram through to Sir Gordon from San Diego, it will give him a chance to be on the lookout," remarked Blake.

"I suppose there is no doubt that he will make for Wu Ling," ventured Tinker.

"I can't imagine what else he would do," rejoined Blake, a little testily. "The Ling-tse vase isn't something one can hawk about among the antique shops. And if a Chinaman tried a game like that his life wouldn't be worth a moment's purchase. Besides, there is probably not a single Chinaman living who doesn't hold the Ling-tse vase in the greatest awe and reverence. No, wherever Chan has made for, you may rest assured it is to pass on the vase to his master, who, in my opinion, can only be Wu Ling. That is unless —"

"Unless what, sir?"

"Unless it is possible that Chan may be in the service of one of the other leaders in China, of whom Sir Gordon spoke. But the chances are more in favour of it being Wu Ling. I should like to know just where Sir Gordon has located the prince."

"Well, it would have needed a submarine or a diving-suit to locate him the last I saw of him," put in Tinker, with a grin of reminiscence. "Honestly, guv'nor, I thought that was the end of Wu

Ling at last. He must have been picked up by one of those other fishing vessels."

"Undoubtedly, if Sir Gordon has located him. At the same time, he must be under the impression that the Ling-tse vase is lost for good. I can only think it must have been in his possession at the time of the explosion, and in some way became wrenched away from him. If that happened while he was in the water, then he must still look upon it as lost. It would be interesting to know what he is figuring on doing now. But we shall know that all right if Chan gets through to him, and tells him how he found the vase. Curious —one of the most curious things that ever happened to me in my life, Tinker.

"It makes me feel as if, in some way, our destiny was irrevocably bound up with that vase. There is something about the whole business that makes me keener to follow up the whole affair than on almost no other occasion in the past. If I were a clairvoyant, I should say that I have a feeling that we are to go through some very strange experiences before we get to the end —if ever we do."

Without being clairvoyant, Blake was right in the presentiment which he had at that moment. And if he had only known how right that presentiment was, even he might have held back, if not for his own sake, then for that of the lad. But Fate had plucked them up, and they were destined to go on once more along that trail of intrigue and mystery, of death and torture.

At San Diego, Blake sent a long code telegram to Sir Gordon Saddler, after which he and Tinker took a hurried meal at the hotel. Then they drove to the station, and caught the night express for Los Angeles, choosing the shore route, as they would continue on through to San Francisco. They managed to secure a private drawing-room, as the private compartments on the American pullmans are known; and since they were both tired after the strenuous day they had been through, they turned in early.

They reached San Francisco without incident, and it had just turned ten o'clock in the morning when they took their way through Chinatown to the house of Hsui-fsi, the mystery man of 'Frisco —the House of the Silver Moon, for it must be remembered that less than half-a-dozen living persons knew that Hsui-fsi, the ancient Celestial of 'Frisco's Chinatown, was, in reality, an English baronet.

They found Sir Gordon seated, just as they had last seen him, on the wide cushion-piled divan in his inner sanctuary. Garbed in his richly-embroidered robe and trousers, he looked as much like a yellow idol as ever; and each time he saw him Blake found it necessary to remind himself that this old man, with his bare, bony skull, and his thin, claw-like hands, was not, after all, what he appeared to be.

As usual, Sir Gordon was smoking one of his eternal yellow cigarettes, which Blake suspected, and rightly, were flavoured with opium, for, he reflected a little sadly, the old man still was marked by the accursed scar of the East, and that now he would never give up the solace he found in it until death claimed him. But it was plain that he had not recently been on one of his heavy bouts, for his eyes were clear and his hand steady as he greeted them.

As usual, a boy entered almost at once with a long, narrow, lacquered tray, on which had been placed a pot of fine Suchow tea, some Santok almonds, a decanter of whisky, and another decanter of soda, with, finally, a big silver box of Egyptian cigarettes, free from any opium flavouring. When Blake and Tinker had been served the old man said:

"Well, well, my friend Blake, we weren't very successful in our last little effort to lay the prince by the heels. You had bad luck. If it hadn't been for that explosion you would have nabbed him. It looks to me as if there had been crooked work of some sort on board."

"It certainly looks that way, Sir Gordon. Tinker, who managed to get aboard the craft, saw nothing out of the way even up to the moment when he was trying to escape from some of Wu Ling's men, who had followed him up the rigging. In fact, the explosion seemed to occur just as he struck the water.

"I was watching through a pair of marine glasses from the converted t.b.d., and saw Tinker drop from the spanker gaff after signalling to me. Then the explosion came, but I cannot say more than that. With dusk coming on, it was impossible to locate Wu Ling among those scores of swimming Chinese, so we were forced to give it up.

"But that is all past now. It is of great importance that you have discovered the whereabouts of Wu Ling and, as you know, I have ascertained for a certainty that the Ling-tse vase was not lost at the time, nor has Wu Ling got it."

"I was very interested to get your telegram last night, Blake. How did you find that the vase was not lost?"

Briefly Blake related how he had spied the flash of blue in the stomach of the tarpon, and how the Chinese boy had managed to secure it under their very eyes by clever sleight-of-hand work, and had afterwards made good his escape.

The old man was highly interested in the story, and chuckled several times during the progress of telling.

"That is why I telegraphed you," went on Blake. "I thought it would be as well if you sent out word to your men to be on the look-out for Chan."

"So I did —so I did, Blake. But I have disappointing news for you. Firstly, Wu Ling is gone —got clean away, and fooled my men in a manner that ought not to have fooled a baby. On top of that, your man Chan has cleared out by way of the gulf. Where he is bound for I cannot say exactly, but I have an idea. One thing I do know, and that is he is not trying to reach Wu Ling. He is not a member of the Brotherhood of the Yellow Beetle."

"What are his intentions, then, Sir Gordon?"

"Just a minute, my boy. One thing at a time. Don't forget my eighty-eight, years. My mind isn't greased as smoothly as yours. Let us take Wu Ling first. I located him yesterday morning. He was in hiding at the house of a certain merchant here, who is high in the councils of the Brotherhood. I immediately threw a cordon about the place, and, by all the points I could count on, it didn't look as if Wu Ling could get through it. But he did, and I will tell you how.

"This morning it became known that he was gone. My men couldn't figure out how he could have managed it. Not a single person or inanimate object had passed in or out of that building without being closely scrutinised by them. I am not blaming them. They are good men, and as cunning as any of their race. But the modern Celestial is not up to all the tricks of the older generation, and Wu Ling didn't find it very difficult to fool them. He chose a simple method which made it all the safer. Ever see a Chinese acrobat at work?" asked Sir Gordon, with apparent irrelevancy.

Both Blake and Tinker nodded.

"Well, like all Celestials who live the austere life which Wu Ling follows; he is extraordinarily supple. In China I have seen —and I dare say you have, too —acrobats who can fold themselves up, so to say, and pack themselves away in an extraordinarily small compass of space. When I had received an itemised account of everything that had passed out of the building in which Wu Ling was hiding, I came to the conclusion that he had evaded my men by adopting just that method, for among the objects which were carried out of the building were several chests of tea. Well, when I found that Wu Ling was no longer there, and, since he hadn't been identified with any of the persons who came out openly, I figured things out; and, while, of course, I am not certain, I am willing to wager a good round sum that one of those chests contained Wu Ling, folded up just as I have said."

"Entirely possible," remarked Blake thoughtfully. "I have also seen the spectacle you mentioned. I believe you are right, Sir Gordon."[4]

"That is not quite all about the prince," continued Sir Gordon. "In some way I am certain he has heard about the finding of the vase. The network of the Brotherhood's agents is extremely well organised on this coast; and I am equally certain that he knew before he escaped from his hiding-place that the finder had managed to get clear through the Gulf of California.

"At any rate, I can tell you for a fact that Prince Wu Ling sailed for China this afternoon by a Japanese liner. For that reason I believe that he has reason to know that the Celestial, who is now in possession of the vase, is also on his way to China."

"H'm! That certainly complicates matters," muttered Blake. "Where do you place the fellow Chan, Sir Gordon? You have intimated that he is not a member of the Brotherhood of the Yellow Beetle."

"Nor is he. If he had been he would have made direct for 'Frisco, to hand the vase over to Wu Ling. When you were here last, Blake, I told you something of what I know to be going on behind the curtain of mystery and intrigue which shuts off China from the western world. I am not prepared to say at present just what strings I myself am pulling there, but Wu Ling is by no means the only person who is fighting for political control of that unfortunate country.

"With one exception, Wu Ling is the most powerful candidate,

---

[4] Author's Note: The method used by Wu Ling to escape from hiding is not only possible, but, to a supple Celestial, would present no difficulty whatever. The writer has, personally seen a Chinese acrobat fold himself up, as it were, and pack himself away into a space considerably smaller than would be contained in a full-sized tea-chest, though not quite so small as that occupied by a "half-chest."

and with that sacred Ling-tse vase in his possession he would sweep everything before him, would have all the north and the south at his feet. But while he does not possess that vase there is another, who, in a religions way —and that, too, means political in China —is equally as powerful.

"He claims to have a better right to the vase than Wu Ling, and he has been scheming for many moons to discover its whereabouts. It is to him that I suspect the fellow Chan has gone.

"If he has, and if he succeeds in delivering the vase into his master's hands, then Heaven help China! The yellow dragon will be torn from jaw to tail, the carcass will be hammered into pulp."

"Who is this person of whom you speak?"

"I speak of the Chuen-to-yan, of the Temple of Eternal Light, in Canton, the mummified devil who has sat on the throne of Eternal Light for a hundred and fifty years; who wields more secret power than any other man in China, unless it be Wu Ling and one other —I speak of him who is at one and the same time the Chuen-to-yan of the Temple of Eternal Light, the august lord of the Brotherhood of the Tiger, and the traditional chief of the sinister Thieves' Market, of Canton, than which slimy organisation there never has been, or ever will be, conceived one more loathsome."

"I have heard of the Chuen-to-yan, of the Temple of Eternal Light," remarked Blake when Sir Gordon had fallen back somewhat exhausted from the vehemence of his words. "But you have spoken of still a third, who may rank as powerful as Wu Ling or the Chuen-to-yan. Am I correct in thinking this third person is yourself, Sir Gordon, he who is known among the Chinese as the ancient and wise and ever-to-be-respected Hsui-fsi?"

No Celestial's eyes ever puckered more obliquely than did Sir Gordon's at that moment. It was uncanny to see how much of the very soul of the East he had acquired during that mysterious half century he had spent in China. He nodded his head, as if he were the yellow god Mo acquiescing in the petition of a worshipper. His reply in English was ridiculously incongruous.

"Yes," he admitted, "I am that third person."

"Then it is as essential for you to recover the Ling-tse vase as if is for us to prevent either Wu Ling or the Chuen-to-yan from getting possession of it. It is only with the vase in your care that China can be kept within bounds. It is only you, Sir Gordon, who can tell the right moment to bring it into effect —who can possibly know into whose hands it should eventually be placed."

"True, my boy. And I have given due thought to all that. Likewise, I have come to a decision. We leave for China to-night!"

Blake laughed a little.

"We!" he echoed. "Does that include us, Sir Gordon?"

The old man lighted another cigarette.

"It does, Blake. It means you and the lad. You have spent too much time over this business to pass it up now. You will not refuse me?"

"I cannot, Sir Gordon. Besides, the Ling-tse vase seems, in some confounded way, to be mixed up in my destiny. I think I shall have to say yes, and to add that I am ready to leave to-night, if you so desire it."

And in those few cool words Sexton Blake made for himself and his assistant Tinker one of the weightiest decisions of his whole career.

ALMOST in the heart of the Shameen, or Foreign Concession of Canton, stands the Eastern Hotel.

It is not quite so large, or fashionable, as the Victoria, but the experienced traveller on the China coast usually chooses it in preference to the latter on account of the beautiful garden it possesses.

From the front of the place this is scarcely visible, but when one passes through the palm court, and the so-called winter garden to the rear, one discovers a centuries-old sylvan retreat which is indescribably pleasant after the smells and noise and dirt of the native town.

It is from there, too, that one has an uninterrupted view of the Peak of Purity, as the Chinese term the distant mountain which can be glimpsed, but which is better known to foreigners as White Cloud Mountain.

During the season of the south-west monsoon, which begins in May and runs on to October, Canton is sticky and humid, and altogether a place to be avoided. But in between seasons —from October to December and from February to May —the climate is delightful, exactly similar to that of Hong Kong. And it is in the early-morning hours, during those balmy months, that the ancient garden of the Eastern Hotel is to be seen at its best.

Standing in the rear porch of the hotel, one looks upon what appears to be a dense tangle of jungle, which one would find difficult to penetrate. But if one had taken the trouble to follow in the footsteps of a certain robust-looking young European very early one morning in the month of November one would have made several interesting discoveries.

The night dew was still shimmering on the leaves, and the birds were still filling the sweet morning air with their joyous carols, when the young man in question stepped easily off the porch and started along a rock-bordered path that seemed to stop at the very fringe of the garden.

But this was only apparently so, for as he turned sharply beneath a moss-covered grotto of rough stone, he found himself in a narrower path which twisted and wound through the dense green in a most bewildering fashion. It was very evident that the young man had passed that way before, for he showed no signs of uncertainty of the direction he should take, even when the narrow path met several other paths, which, to the uninitiated, would have been puzzling.

He had penetrated some little distance into the maze when he came suddenly upon a small pagoda garden house in which a richly-clad Chinese gentleman was sipping his morning cup of Suchow tea. The European lad knew him for a very wealthy banker from the north, and after the custom of the country, he paused and salaamed courteously to the elder one.

The latter gravely returned the salute, and in quite good English bade the Westerner the top of the morning in numerous flowery phrases. The young man responded with due respect, after which he again salaamed and passed on.

The little pagoda was soon lost to view as he got deeper into the maze, but the beauty of his surroundings increased, if that were possible, for, a little later, the sweetest of silvery tinkles reached his ears, and presently he stepped out of a lovely green arbour to find himself at the edge of a tiny stream which was singing away gaily as it tumbled along over its stony bed.

But it was not the stream which had caused that sharp, silvery tinkle he had heard. The sound was now just above him, and as he lifted his eyes he saw attached to the branch of a tree close to him several strips of painted glass which were being stirred ever so gently by the faint breath of the morning.

It was the bits of glass striking together that caused the sound —a guard to keep at bay any evil spirits which might have passed that way during the night.

On his left was a narrow teakwood bridge which spanned the little stream. It was built in a very high arch, typical of Eastern bridge architecture, and its ancient rails were completely concealed by the tangled green vines which hung in heavy clouds, as if their tips were seeking to drink from the gay little silvery stream.

The young man stood for a few minutes breathing in the fresh beauty of his surroundings, then he turned and mounted the steep slope of the bridge. He paused again on the crest of the arch to gaze down into the brook; then, whistling softly to himself, he descended to the other side and plunged into another narrow path there. The way was less distinctly marked on this side, but that troubled the young man not at all, for he showed not the slightest hesitation in choosing the way he should go.

For all the sound that reached him from the outside world, he might have been in the depths of actual jungle. The only human soul he had seen since leaving the hotel had been the elderly gentleman in his vividly-coloured robes, sipping his amber tea and communing reverently with the past. Yet the old man fitted completely into the picture, and, if anything at all was incongruous, it was the young one clad in the garments of the West.

Deeper and deeper he went until he passed another small pagoda, at the back of which was a deserted shrine, and above which also tinkled a few strips of devil glass. But now, so dense was the overgrowth of green, the blue of the morning sky was scarcely visible, and the sun's oblique rays failed completely to reach the path which the young man trod.

He turned to the right by the pagoda, and then sharply to the left, which brought him directly under a very ancient and wide-spreading choman tree. Then again he took the right, after which he went straight ahead until, as he parted a leafy wall in front of him, he came upon a high wall, which was completely covered by dense vines.

So thick were they that it would have been plain to the least observant, several hundreds of years must have been necessary for their slow growth to achieve such venerable density.

The young man kept along close to the wall until he came to a place where the wall was bare of vines, and where, no one knows how long ago, a massive iron and copper studded teak door had been fitted. It revealed no sign of either lock or handle, but high up was a heavy iron knocker. This the young man lifted and let fall once, twice, thrice. He stood waiting for a few seconds, and then, without warning of any kind, the great door swung open away from him.

In the aperture stood an old Chinaman, who salaamed low as he stood aside for the European to enter.

The young man stepped through, and the door closed behind him.

He found himself in a dense and venerable garden which might have been a part of the one he had just left. Over the tops of the trees he could just glimpse the pagoda roof of a large building some distance away.

As a matter of fact, away back in the days when the Manchus first poured through with their Tartar mercenaries into the north, that garden in which the lad now stood had been almost as venerable as it was on this sunny morning.

Then, too, it had been identified with the one he had just left, for at that time the building which forms the main part of the Eastern Hotel was the house of the military governor of Canton, while the pagoda-like structure which the young man could see above the trees had been the house of the Lord High August One of Two Hundred Intelligences, the two houses sharing the vast garden jointly, with the exception of a lattice dividing-fence, which had later been replaced by the wall of feudal strength.

As he had shown familiarity with the garden he had first penetrated, so did the young man now reveal a knowledge of the second one. He set off along a path, and, after numerous twistings and turnings, came to another part of the same little stream which he had crossed before. Once more he passed over a high-pitched bridge spanning it, and, after descending, made his way along until he came to a pagoda not unlike the one where the elderly gentleman from the north had been drinking his tea.

And this pagoda, like the other, had its occupant —or, rather, occupants —for as the young man reached the open front he caught sight of two other richly clad gentlemen engaged in the same pleasant occupation of sipping the amber liquid which can only be made a perfect brew with the finest of Suchow.

One of these gentlemen was very old, although his eyes were clear and full of an active intelligence. The other, much younger, looked like a prosperous member of the mandarin class, although his high brow and breadth of skull gave an impression of studious gravity which one might acquire from a long and careful study of the five classics.

It was rather strange to find a European youth coming upon two such typically Chinese gentlemen in such a quiet retreat, whither not one European would find his way in, perhaps, twenty years.

But the youth seemed unabashed at the discovery. Nor, strange to say, did the two gentlemen appear in the least perturbed at the interruption. On the contrary, the elder of the two lifted a hand in greeting, while the younger gave a nod and made a gesture for the youth to be seated.

The young man dropped down, and, after accepting a cup of the fragrant Suchow, which was handed to him by a Chinese boy, who seemed to pop out of the very ground and disappear as magically, lighted a cigarette. But it was the younger of the two men who spoke first.

"Anything to report, my lad?"

"Not a thing, guv'nor," responded the youth. "I had a short talk last night with Li-Chu-Sen, the banker, as Sir Gordon suggested. He has promised to try to discover if Wu Ling is actually in Canton, and if he does he is going to let me know. He hasn't succeeded in doing so yet, for I passed him on my way here, and he said nothing. As soon as it is safe he would like to come through here and have a talk with you and Sir Gordon."

"We shall try to arrange that for this evening," said the elderly gentleman, who was, as may have been gathered by now, in reality, Sir Gordon Saddler. "But it will not be necessary for him to make those inquiries, for we have had news since yesterday."

Tinker —for the lad was he —sat up with an exclamation of interest. "Something important, sir?"

"Yes," said Blake. "Wu Ling is in Canton, and we know where he will be at eleven o'clock this morning. It will be necessary for you to be there as well, my lad. Now, listen while I outline the plans we have just made."

BEFORE detailing further exactly what the plan was which Sexton Blake and Sir Gordon Saddler had evolved, it will be as well, perhaps, to explain briefly just how it came about that the mystery man of 'Frisco and Blake were living at the house of the Lord High August One of the Two Hundred Intelligences, disguised as two high-class Chinese gentlemen, while Tinker, quite undisguised, was living at the Eastern Hotel, the garden of which abutted on that at the rear of the place of the extremely Celestial name.

Once the decision had been arrived at in San Francisco that the trio should leave for Canton, no time was lost in putting it into effect. It transpired that a Pacific mail-steamer was leaving the day following the return of Blake and Tinker to 'Frisco, and it had been possible to book passages by this ship.

Before sailing, Sir Gordon had received further information from his numerous spies which appeared to confirm his theory that Wu Ling had escaped from his hiding-place inside a tea-chest, and just before they left the House of the Silver Moon they received definite confirmation that he had sailed for China by a Japanese liner.

Of the elusive Chan they heard nothing more, but Blake was inclined to agree with the wise old man that nothing was more likely than that he was on his way to China. This move on Chans part seemed also to strengthen Sir Gordon's theory that he was the servant of the Chuen-to-yan, of the Temple of Eternal Light, rather than of the stormy petrel of China, Prince Wu Ling.

At any rate, all the signs pointed to Canton as being the next spot on which their attention should be focussed. If Chan had made for there with the vase, then it was pretty safe betting that Wu Ling would also go there. Whether the prince would find it possible to overtake Chan and force him to give up the vase was a moot question.

During their numerous conversations on board ship Sir Gordon had revealed to Blake a good deal of secret history regarding the Chuen-to-yan which was new to Blake. But, from what Sir Gordon did tell him, it was easy to understand that, in his way, the powerful head of all the Buddhists was as mighty as Wu Ling, and in the gigantic struggle which was now going on in China for supreme power he would be able to employ as many resources as the prince.

Further than that, both Blake and Tinker gained a considerable insight into the mysterious power wielded by Sir Gordon himself, and, although the mysterious old man was reticent on many points, it was plain that he felt on pretty solid ground, since he was courageous enough to pit himself against both Wu Ling and the Chuen-to-yan.

It was a triangle of intrigue which promised a good deal, and Blake realised that they would need to employ every resource at their command if they were to come through it. Hence the care they had exercised on their arrival in Canton.

The house of the Lord High August One of Two Hundred Intelligences had been for many years the property of Sir Gordon. Originally it had come to him through the Chinese princess whom he had married, and who had inherited from several generations of previous owners connected with her own mother's family.

They had quietly installed themselves there, and as Blake was fluently conversant with many of the Chinese dialects, of which Cantonese was one, and since he had on other occasions lived as a Celestial in the very heart of the Canton bazaar, there was little difficulty in arranging the necessary disguise. And since their retreat abutted on the garden of the Eastern Hotel, Tinker had been instructed to take up his quarters there.

For the present the lad had posed simply as a tourist, and while he had not shown himself about conspicuously, he had nevertheless been able to keep in close touch with the foreign life of the Shameen, which was essential in their plans. He it was who reported each morning to Blake and Sir Gordon, and though he made no effort to disguise himself while in the hotel, he nevertheless assumed a simple plan whenever he went abroad which was sufficient for his purpose.

The manager of the Eastern Hotel was a friend of Blake's, and as the hotel land was also the property of Sir Gordon there was not much risk of betrayal through him. On the other hand, just as it was possible for Sir Gordon and Blake to find out about Wu Ling's movements, so was it possible for the prince to discover that they were in Canton, nor would any disguise prevent that. It had all simply boiled down to a case of which could outwit the other.

What Blake and Sir Gordon proposed was the first step in this direction, and while Tinker sat puffing his cigarette, Blake outlined the plan.

"It is simply this, my lad," he said. "Through his system of information, Sir Gordon has discovered that Wu Ling is in Canton. In fact, he has discovered quite a lot more about the movements of the prince; but the point most germane to the plan we have formed is that we know where Wu Ling is to be at eleven o'clock this morning."

"That is something definite to go on, anyway," put in Tinker. "Where is he to be, guv'nor?"

"You know the Thieves' Market, my lad?"

"I should say so," responded Tinker, with a grin. "Don't you remember the dust-up I had there the last time we were here?"

"That was in my mind when I spoke," answered Blake dryly, while Sir Gordon chuckled. "Therefore, you will have no difficulty in finding it! Just beyond the Thieves' Market, Tinker, is the Gate of the Tiger, which, as you know, leads out of Canton proper to the quarter of the Tatars. Now, just inside that gate is a jade shop, which you will recall, for we both visited it on one occasion."

"Yes, sir. I remember it perfectly."

"Very good. Almost opposite the jade shop is a small temple known as the Temple of Ancient Virtues. From the street it is impossible to see the full extent of this building, owing to the triple pagoda roof; but, last evening, just before the hour of rice, Sir Gordon took me up on to the roof of a certain building not far from the Thieves' Market, From there I was able to see that the rear wall of the Temple of Ancient Virtues abuts on to the rear wall of the great Temple of Eternal Light. In fact, it forms a sort of chapel, so to say, of the larger one.

"There are further details connected with those two buildings which it is not necessary for you to know at present. What will guide you is the fact that Prince Wu Ling is due at the Temple of Ancient Virtues this morning, at the hour I have named. What is his purpose in going there, we do not know. It may be simply a pilgrimage of worship.

"But, on the other hand, in view of the fact that we now believe the Chuen-to-yan, of the Temple of Eternal Light, is in possession of the Ling-tse vase, and since there is, undoubtedly, secret means of communication from the Temple of Ancient Virtues to the underground secret rooms where the Chuen-to-yan spends all his time, we think it reasonable to imagine that Wu Ling may be going to a private rendezvous with the Chuen-to-yan. If that should prove to be the case, then there is scarcely any doubt that the prince will try to come to some arrangement regarding the vase with the Chuen-to-yan.

Do you follow me?"

"Perfectly, sir!"

"Very good! Now, it is up to you to make for the Thieves' Market, and go on to the jade shop of which I spoke. I would suggest that you adopt some simple form of disguise. It will be safer not to overdo it, for there will be plenty of spies on the look-out on Wu Ling's behalf. You must bear in mind every single moment that we are trying to pilot our course through a place that is honeycombed with intrigue, and that we have two known factions to deal with, which, we have had proof, are capable of going to any lengths, and particularly so here in Canton, where their deeds will not be questioned. Were it not for the third powerful organisation controlled by Sir Gordon, we wouldn't stand a chance.

"Therefore, you can see how vitally important it is that we should know what is afoot between Wu Ling and the Chuen-to-yan."

"I quite see that, sir," interposed Tinker gravely, for he realised only too well that Blake was not over-painting the seriousness of the case. "I take it, then, that I am to try to find out as much as I can about Wu Ling's movements after he reaches the little temple of which you spoke."

"Exactly! Also, to bear in mind that you are to avoid being discovered by the prince. Watch when he enters the Temple of Ancient Virtues —mark the time when he emerges; then come back to report at once; for on that report we can perhaps come to some conclusion, and thus take the next step."

"Very good, sir! By the way, guv'nor, what shall I say to Li-Chu-Sen if he is still in the pagoda when I return?"

Blake turned towards Sir Gordon.

"What will he say, Sir Gordon?"

"If he is in the pagoda there this evening, at dusk, I think we can manage to send a servant through to guide him here. Will you tell him that, Tinker?"

"Yes, sir. And now I think I had better be off. I have a few things to arrange before I start out."

"Well, bear in mind what I have said. Tinker," urged Blake.

"Never fear, guv'nor! I'll keep my peepers open!"

And with that Tinker tossed away the end of his cigarette and rose, waving his hand as he started back the way he had come.

CHINA is probably the only country in the world where one may find an organised and recognised, Thieves' Market, such as exists in Canton, Peking, and other cities of the yellow republic.

It seems a strange idea that the profession of thieving should be regarded as a highly-to-be-desired career, in which those who follow it are looked upon with no little respect by their fellows. But such indeed is the case, and it follows, as a matter of course, that these gentry find it necessary to have a well-organised clearing centre for their ill-gotten —or, as they regard it, well-gotten —gains.

The Thieves' Market in Canton is not so large as that at Peking, but it serves its purpose for a community which numbers more than a million in the city proper, while the adjacent river population might be put at another half-million without one being very far astray.

There is no street in the native town of Canton that is not about the last word in dirt, noise, and smells; but if there is any bedrock at all in that noisome hole, one would probably find it in the Thieves' Market, although some of the riverside quarters would run it pretty close.

Tourists sometimes penetrate to the fringe of this part, and regard it from afar with either a touch of nervousness or amusement, according to their temperament. But a few, very few, Europeans have gone down beneath the crust, and some of the things they found could not be described in print. It is not only a clearing-house for the regular gains of the thieving profession, but it is in the very deepest strata of vice.

Of those who had penetrated deeply into the place were Sexton Blake and Tinker and Blake had had no difficulty at all in recalling the "dust-up" which the lad had had there. Tinker referred to it now in jocular terms; but at the time it had been touch and go whether he would get out of the place alive, and the experience had served to make him decidedly cautious on subsequent visits to Canton.

Tinker was never unwilling to "mix" things as they came along, but he wasn't quite so hungry for trouble as to seek it willingly in the Thieves' Market of Canton. It can be understood, therefore, that on this morning, when he started out to get track of Wu Ling, he carried himself with considerable circumspection as he approached the vicious quarter.

Tinker was clad in ordinary European clothes, or rather, in clothes having an American cut. Over his close-cropped head of dark hair, he had placed a snugly-fitting wig of fair hair, which was plastered down flat. When he had finished this off with a small blonde moustache, he had achieved a far more effective disguise than would have been the case, had he indulged in more elaborate measures.

He looked considerably older, and entirely different from the young man who had been about the Eastern Hotel for the past few days. On his head he wore a wide-brimmed Panama hat, while over one shoulder he had swung a kodak. He looked exactly like a young man seeing the world, who had taken the trouble to run up from Hong Kong to investigate Canton.

And that was exactly the impression Tinker wished to create.

He left the hotel in a chair, but, as he passed through the street of the brass workers and turned past the silk bazaar, he ordered his carriers to stop. He got out there, and, after paying them off, proceeded on foot through the lace bazaar, until he came to the outer fringe of the better-known streets. He knew now that he was getting close to the Thieves' Market, and kept moving ahead at an even pace as he began to pass through the quarter which he must traverse to reach the Temple of Ancient Virtues.

It strikes one as rather a humorous sidelight on the profession of thieving in China that among the most devoted adherents of the Temple of Ancient Virtues were the inhabitants of the Thieves' Market.

Outwardly, there was nothing to distinguish the quarter from any of the other more disreputable districts of Canton. The streets were lined with small shops, displaying a variety of wares of every description, while above the shops were the mean-looking rickety upper parts where a teeming life existed.

But Tinker knew that, probably at that very moment, a thousand or more transactions were taking place among the underground cellars and passages with which the quarter is honeycombed, ranging in nature from a shrieking haggle over a bit of Swatow lace to the disposal of a human slave for the rice-fields in the interior. There is not supposed to be slavery in China, but there is plenty of it on a well-organised scale.

No one paid any attention to him as he passed along. If any of their former enemies, or of Wu Ling's scattered spies, had recognised him, it is safe to say that, even in broad daylight, there would have been another mysterious disappearance of a European. But, as he appeared to be simply a tourist, it was a risky business to stir up the foreign embassies. So he was permitted to proceed in peace.

Tinker revealed not the slightest sign that he knew he was going through a dangerous quarter. He went ahead with perfect sang froid until he came in sight of the massive Gate of the Tiger. A little later he saw the jade shop, which was jammed up against one of the ancient pillars of the wall, and then across from it, as Blake had said, he caught sight of a pagoda-like structure, which he knew must be the Temple of Ancient Virtues.

Glancing at his wrist watch, Tinker saw that it was just a few minutes after half-past ten, which means that he had still plenty of time before Wu Ling was due to put in an appearance.

He slowed down a little now, and, on reaching the jade shop, paused outside on the pretext of looking about him. In reality, he was making a swift survey of the entrance to the temple to assure himself where and how Wu Ling must make his entry. Then he entered, and began to occupy himself by examining the trays of jade which had been laid out inside the shop.

Tinker was no expert in jade, but Sexton Blake, who had built up one of the finest collections in Europe, had taught him quite a little about the beautiful pink and green stone which comes out of China, and he had remembered sufficient to proceed intelligently in an examination of the wares before him.

Some of the stuff was poor, laid out to catch the roving eye of the ignorant tourist. But, when the lad had contemptuously waved these trays aside, the old Chinaman who owned the place soon produced his better quality.

Tinker made a small purchase of green plaque, after a considerable amount of haggling which he deliberately prolonged; then he moved towards the door, and gave his attention to another tray on which were some rather fine pink shafts. He was thus engaged when a glance at his wrist-watch showed him that it lacked just two minutes of eleven.

So, moving still closer to the door, as if to get a better light on one of the shafts, he was able, under this pretext, to keep a watch on the road outside. And, sharp at eleven o'clock, a rich-looking equipage appeared.

Whatever Wu Ling may have known about the movements of Sexton Blake and Sir Gordon Saddler, it was plain that this knowledge would not cause him to make any secret of his own movements, which proved how utterly safe he felt in Canton. It showed Tinker, too, that, even if Sir Gordon's agents had not been able to secure their information before, they would have had no difficulty in doing so that day.

The carriage was a low one with a driver and footman on the box. Both men were garbed after the fashion of the Tartar races, and Tinker's experienced eye soon discerned that the horses were no scrub beasts from South China. They showed, too, plainly the marks of the thoroughbred of the northern steppes.

Wu Ling himself was in the carriage, dressed in formal and rich garments, the most striking of which was the heavily-embroidered tunic of imperial yellow. Even at the distance, Tinker could see the gleam of the great yellow topaz with which it was caught together.

On his head the prince wore one of the small caps which only true Manchu royalty may wear, and on his austere countenance was a faint expression of stern contempt for the rabble through which his escort drove a way, and which salaamed to the ground as he passed, despite the fact that China was supposed to be a republic.

Wu Ling was one of the "Heaven born" of the old dynasty, and that was enough for the mob.

The horses were brought up before the Temple of Ancient Virtues with a flourish, the silver bells on their bridles tinkling musically as they tossed their heads. Then the footman sprang down, and, as he opened the door of the carriage —on which Tinker could discern Wu Li rig's princely cipher —he bent almost to the ground in humble obeisance as the prince stepped out.

Tinker watched while the prince entered the temple, then, as the carriage drove off, he laid the piece of jade back on the tray, and, after a few words with the old Celestial, strolled out. He was not very much in fear that he would attract much attention, for it was no unusual sight to see a tourist in the vicinity of some one of the numerous temples, and Tinker heightened the effect by taking his kodak from its case and focussing it on the temple.

He took a couple of snapshots, after which, still carrying the camera in his hand, he made his way across the narrow street and entered the building.

Tinker had never been in the Temple of Ancient Virtues, but he found it not unlike several others which he had entered. The outside and interior architecture were typically Chinese, the inner hall being a high-pitched vaulted place with a score or more of massive pillars supporting it. These pillars and the walls were almost entirely covered with strange arabesques, and fantastic representations of various forms of Chinese torture, while, interspersed among the whole, were patches of vivid colouring —pink and gold and green, yellow and brown and crimson, mauve and black and orange —giving a startling and bizarre effect, and yet not at all unpleasing.

Though the interior was dim, Tinker could discern a high, carved stone screen at the far end, behind which he knew were the shrines of various gods, and, as he could see nothing of Wu Ling, he thought the prince must have passed behind this screen.

Tinker paused about half-way up the temple, and, under pretext of studying the fantastic drawings on one of the pillars, mulled the thing over in his mind.

"The guv'nor said to watch from the jade shop, and note when Wu Ling entered and when he came out," he said to himself. "Well, that is easier said than done. If Wu Ling is really going to a rendezvous with the mysterious Chuen-to-yan of whom the guv'nor spoke, then, it stands to reason, he will be occupied a considerable time —that is, if the two yellow devils hatch up some sort of an alliance.

"Well, if I hang about that jade shop for so long it is bound to rouse suspicion. You can bet that Wu Ling didn't come here in all that pomp without knowing that there would be scores of the members of the Brotherhood of the Yellow Beetle hanging about to safeguard him, for he can't know yet how the Chuen-to-yan will receive him, and Wu Ling is altogether too cunning a bird to take any chances.

"So, that being so, I guess I wouldn't be out there long before I was spotted. If I was I would have about as much chance of remaining there as a canary would have of discussing the weather with a hungry tomcat.

"On the other hand, it is going to be a mighty ticklish business trying to find out just where Wu Ling has gone. He may or may not have gone behind that screen. There may be a passage from there into the underground apartments of the Temple of Eternal Light, where his nibs, the good old Chuen-to-yan, hangs out. But what price me? If I go poking about behind that screen I am just as liable as not to get my ribs tickled up with the point of a knife. These yellow boys don't like the foreign devils poking about the holy of holies of one of their temples, or whatever it is they call 'em.

"And if I butted into Wu Ling it wouldn't take him long to see through this nice blonde wig and dinky little moustache I am wearing. Then what to do?

"Hallo! Who is this old codger coming from behind the screen? He looks ancient enough to be the Chuen-to-yan himself, whom Sir Gordon says is believed to be more than a hundred and fifty years old. It seems a crazy idea, but, from what the guv'nor has told me, you never can tell how long some of these old ascetics might hang on. I'll bet he's not the Chuen-toodly-oodly, but I guess I am not far off if I put him down as one of the temple priests. I'll tackle him, anyway, and see if half a dozen pieces of silver won't get me permission to poke about a bit longer."

With this in his mind Tinker moved forward and stood waiting until the ancient Celestial approached. Then the lad made a sign of deep respect, as one should to the aged. The priest returned the salutation and came to a stop.

Now Tinker could rattle off the Cantonese dialect fairly fluently, but he knew no ordinary tourist would be supposed to possess that knowledge, so he was on his guard. He addressed the priest in the dialect, but in a few short, stilted phrases, parrot fashion, which, would give the impression that he had primed himself with a few useful sentences before visiting Canton.

Apparently the priest was not altogether a stranger to tourists and such requests, for he was as slick as a juggler in disposing of the coins which Tinker slipped into his hand; then he smiled a toothless smile. From what he said Tinker gathered that he might roam about the temple for a short time, but that he was not to be permitted to take any photographs was evident, for the old man made him leave his camera on the floor at the foot of the pillar, though how he was expected to make an exposure in that gloomy interior Tinker couldn't guess.

He had expected the old man to accompany him, but he soon found that, for the time being at least, he was to be left to his own resource's, for, after a further salutation, the priest continued on his way to the door.

Tinker knew that he would probably return at any moment, and as he was anxious to have a peep behind the stone screen, he determined to risk it while he seemed to have a chance.

He waited until the old man had passed out to the porch, then he sped forward towards the end of the screen. He made his way round it, and found himself gazing into a dimly-lit place, at the back of which half a dozen large idols —three on each side —flanked a gigantic statue of Dhabutsa, the great Buddha.

As his eyes became more accustomed to the gloom Tinker discerned two massive stone doors let into the rear wall of the temple —one in the far corner on the right, and one almost in front of him. He hesitated. For a few seconds he debated if he would make an attempt to discover what was behind those two doors.

But caution whispered to him not to be precipitate.

He backed away until he was once more in front of the screen in the main hall of the temple. And well was it for him that he did so, for, as he turned slowly round, he saw the aged priest just on the point of coming through the great pillared entrance.

Tinker made for the nearest pillar, and made a pretence of studying the grotesque figures which had been painted on it. Then he passed in a casual manner on to the next, and another, and another, deliberately making his way towards one side, so that he should not be forced to have further conversation with the priest.

Out of the corner of his eyes he saw the priest glance towards him, but, apparently satisfied that the "tourist" was only harmlessly satisfying his curiosity, he kept on his way and disappeared behind the screen.

Tinker slipped round one of the great pillars, and stood listening tensely, he could just distinguish the soft slush-slush, slush-slush of the priest's sandals as he moved across the tiled floor behind the stone screen. Then there came a momentary silence, followed by the sound of the impact of something heavy against something hard. Tinker knew only too well what it meant.

"'The stone door, the one in the far right comer," he muttered. "That means old greybeard has gone into his own quarters. He may be only a few moments, or he may be some time. But, anyway, I can't investigate things in that direction. The only thing left is to see what is behind that other door. I may fall into a pretty mess, but I'll bet Wu Ling went through one of those doors, and I'll try everything once. I'd better get the camera, though, and then, if the old boy pops out and sees the temple empty, he will think I have cleared off."

With that he stole across to the pillar, at the foot of which he had left his kodak. Slipping the strap of the case over his shoulder, he made his way as noiselessly as possible towards the stone screen.

He passed round the end of this, and stole across to the door, which was almost in front of him. There was no sign of lock or bolt, but Tinker had seen such doors before, and reckoned a good pressure on one side would cause it to swing open.

He was right. It swung inwards, and, passing through, he found himself in a dimly-lit passage, which seemed to slope downwards at a sharp angle. The roof was scarcely a foot above his head, but how the place received any light at all he could not fathom until he had turned a sharp bend in the passage, and saw, just above him, a small, heavily-barred window.

He put up his hands and clasped the bars. He drew himself up until he could peer out between the bars. He saw nothing but a narrow, stone-walled well, which he figured must have been built as a light well. He dropped back to his feet and kept on.

"This looks promising," he muttered. "It wouldn't surprise me if I had struck the passage which leads to the subterranean apartments of the Chuen-to-yan. Anyway, I'll go on a bit farther and find out."

It did not take him long to find a change and a puzzle. After two more turnings he came to what appeared to be simply a blank wall — a dead end to the passage. But Tinker knew this could not be the case.

He knew that, in some way, there was a way through; but it was when he lifted up his eyes he discovered the solution.

Just there it was so dimly lighted that he had great difficulty in seeing more than his immediate surroundings. Outside that everything was wrapped in a mysterious and chill gloom. But he was able to make out that, about two feet above his head, there was an opening, and, when he had dragged himself up and scrambled through, he found himself in a second passage.

He got to his feet and stood listening. From somewhere ahead came a faint line of grey light, and, in the distance, he could hear a strange jumble of sound, which eventually resolved itself into the discordant beatings of many gongs.

"Looks as if I was getting somewhere near the Temple of Eternal Light," he thought. "Anyway, I've come so far I'll keep on. It might be useful to the guv'nor and Sir Gordon later to know about this passage into the quarters of the Chuen-to-yan —if that is where it leads."

He started on again, finding that this passage, like the other, went down at a sharp angle. How many times he turned he did not know. But the corners were very frequent, and all the time he knew himself to be getting lower and lower.

Then he came to what puzzled him extremely. In fact, so abruptly did he come upon it that it was nearly his undoing, for he pulled up just in time to find himself at the very edge of a wide hole in the passage he was traversing.

Tinker dropped to his knees and peered through the opening. He could see just beneath him, another passage which appeared to be feebly lit by some sort of yellow illumination. The floor of this new passage was only a matter of six feet or so beneath him, and, without reckoning how he was to get back through the opening, should he so desire, Tinker swung round and dropped through.

He landed lightly, and, as far as he could see, the passage was about the same as the others. Where the yellow light came from he couldn't see; but just ahead of him was a corner, so he made for it.

He turned this, and then, as his heart came into his throat, he backed away in an attempt to retreat. But to save his life, Tinker, for one awful moment, could not have turned his head away from the terrible sight which met his gaze. It was so acutely nauseating to the sense of sight that his whole being was paralysed by the stunning shock of it.

And little wonder is it that for that brief space of time he stood rigid, helpless to move, for never before had he looked upon a more terrible and bestial sight.

Not three feet away from him was one of the most gigantic creatures Tinker had ever seen. He could have been not less than six feet ten in height, and, in that dimly-lit passage, he loomed far greater. He was naked to the waist, his torso and face being painted in vivid yellow with bestial designs.

His arms were outstretched, the huge claw-like hands closing and unclosing as if he were a cliff tiger sheathing and unsheathing its claws. But worse, far, far worse than that was the terrible visage of the being.

The lips had at some time been cut clean away, leaving a gaping orifice in which vicious yellow tusks added a still further bestial touch, to the creature. The lobes of the ears had been dragged down until it had been possible to insert in the openings yellow metal discs as large as ordinary saucers. The nose had been spread by a similar disfiguration, while the eyes —never had Tinker imagined that the orbs of a human being could hold such a terrible blend of evil and murderous malignity as those eyes held.

With a mighty effort Tinker regained control of his shocked nerves. It took the quickest of brain messages to tell him that he had never been nearer death, awful and unspeakable, than at that moment. He had just one chance, and he knew he must take it, and at the very moment when a ghastly, whistling sound was emitted from between those terrible yellow fangs the lad turned to run.

He hadn't even that one chance in a million.

Before he could get back round the bend of the passage the terrible thing had hurled itself forward. For one sickening moment Tinker felt the vile breath of the creature in his disgusted nostrils, then those terrible yellow claws gripped his throat, and he went down in a heap, his outraged jugular throbbing under the pressure of those murderous talons.

" Look, what does that mean ? " asked the disguised Sexton Blake. Sir Gordon followed the direction of the detective's gaze. Two of the approaching Celestials were supporting a third, whose blue tunic was darkened by an ugly stain, which spread as they looked at it. *(Chapter 6.)*

BY the early afternoon both Blake and Sir Gordon were beginning to feel uneasy, but not acutely anxious about Tinker. Allowing for unforeseen delay, they figured that he should have been back to report somewhere around one o'clock, and, in any event, not later than two. But two had come and gone with no sign of the lad. That he had not yet come back to the hotel they knew, for one of Sir Gordon's servants had been sent through the gardens to keep watch for him, and the man had not yet returned.

The two were sitting in the pagoda in the garden smoking, and wondering what could have happened, when suddenly Blake, who was facing the path which led to the house, shot out his hand and touched his companion's arm.

"Look! What does that mean?" he asked sharply.

Sir Gordon followed the direction of Blake's gaze, then he muttered a smothered imprecation. And it is not strange that they were puzzled at what they saw; for, coming along the path towards them were three Celestials, all members of Sir Gordon's system. Two of them were supporting the third between them, and it was plain that the man was in extremis, and the coarse blue tunic had been turned dark by a great spreading stain.

"Wounded, and badly," muttered Blake. "I wonder what has happened?"

"We shall soon know," responded Sir Gordon.

The trio reached them just then, and, as the wounded man was carried into the pavilion he made a supreme effort to hold himself upright. His eyes, already glassy with approaching death, stared almost unseeingly at his master. But as Sir Gordon spoke to him he was sufficiently conscious to recognise the tones.

At once he poured out a hoarse stammering tale which Blake, who was not so close as the baronet, had considerable difficulty in following, although he knew the argot well enough. But Sir Gordon evidently grasped the import of what was said, for, as the man's voice trailed off, he shot out a single tense question.

The man made another effort, succeeded in answering, then his body collapsed like a limp sack, and he slipped through the arms of the pair who held him, falling in a heap at Sir Gordon's feet. It needed the briefest of examinations to show that he was dead. Sir Gordon

38

gravely motioned the other two to take the body away, then he turned to Blake.

"Did you understand?" he asked.

"Some, Sir Gordon; sufficient to tell me that it had to do with Tinker. What was it?"

"Yes, it was about the lad. He is in trouble, serious trouble, Blake. I will explain. As you know, several of my men were on duty in the neighbourhood of the Temple of Ancient Virtues this morning. But, as they were very greatly outnumbered by both Wu Ling's men and men belonging to the Chuen-to-yan, it turned out, as we expected, that they were not able to get near enough to discover just what Wu Ling was doing.

"He was seen to drive along the street which leads past the temple to the Gate of the Tiger; also Tinker was seen to pass that way some time before the prince put in an appearance. Just what happened immediately after that is not quite clear, but apparently the lad followed the prince into the temple.

"From what my unfortunate agent was able to communicate before he died, it seems that Wu Ling came out some time after and drove off. But no signs were seen of the lad. This man who managed to reach us succeeded in getting through the cordon which the Chuen-to-yan had thrown round the place, and —how I don't know — managed, in some way, to discover that Tinker had fallen into the hands of the chief sacrificial priest of the Temple of Eternal Light."

"Good heavens! If that is so, Sir Gordon, it means that he must have penetrated the secret passage leading from the smaller temple to the larger one. And if he is in the hands of the sacrificial priest it means —"

"We know too well what it would mean under ordinary circumstances, Blake. But, the usual course is not to be followed this time. At least, that is what the poor fellow told me before he succumbed. He, too, was found in the temple and was attacked, but, although his wounds were mortal, he still managed to get away and tell us what happened. No; Tinker, it seems, is not to go to the altar of sacrifice, but to a fate far, far worse in many ways. He is to be sold in the Thieves' Market."

Blake jumped to his feet in deep agitation.

"Why, that means he is destined to be sold as a slave for one of the rice-fields somewhere in the interior!" he cried.

"Quite so, Blake! And once he is taken there we shall have very, very slim hopes of rescuing him. Therefore we must act immediately. Unfortunately, we have so little to go on that it is going to be difficult. But if it is so that he is to be sold in the Thieves' Market; then we know where to begin."

"If he goes there it will do no good to notify the foreign consuls," muttered Blake. "No; that is out of the question. Whatever is done must be done independently by us. If any harm comes to the lad, Sir Gordon, I will find my way into the quarters of the Chuen-to-yan and kill him as I would a snake!"

"Steady, my boy!" said the old man. "I know all the workings of that accursed Thieves' Market, Wu Ling and the Chuen-to-yan can command powerful forces, but I have an idea that the bulk of them will be on duty tonight in the neighbourhood of the Temples of Eternal Light. Even if Wu Ling and the Chuen-to-yan have come to an agreement, the Chuen-to-yan will not be so foolish as to relax his guard. Therefore we shall concentrate all our forces on the Thieves' Market. I shall give orders at once for the word to be sent round."

"Do you think Tinker has been taken yet to the Thieves' Market?"

"No, I don't. I fancy he will be taken just after dusk, but of course, the other is quite possible, for I know there is secret underground communication between the Temple of Ancient Virtues and the Market. But I know quite a little about that quarter myself, although it is a great many years since I have descended into it. But, rest assured, Blake, we shall not leave the lad in their hands. As for the Ling-tse vase —well, it will have to wait for the present."

Although Sir Gordon controlled an extensive system in Canton, as well, as in North China, it was no small matter to get together, during the few hours remaining to them, as large a force as both he and Blake knew would be necessary for the purpose they had in view. Nevertheless, it was done; and by dusk that evening Sir Gordon had made his dispositions.

During the afternoon, too, several valuable items of information reached them, among which were that, as far as could be ascertained, Tinker was still a prisoner in the underground apartments of the Temple of Eternal Light, that certain signs within the purlieus of the Thieves' Market pointed to an important occurrence there that night, and that, as Sir Gordon had opined, a strong cordon was being kept posted in the neighbourhood of both the temples —proving that, whether the prince and the Chuen-to-yan had or had not come to any agreement, the wily old priest was not going to give Wu Ling a chance to bring off a coup.

In order to make their plans carry every possible prospect of success, it was essential to ensure a complete control of the Thieves' Market during the time their major operation would be in progress, which might be a matter of minutes or even of hours. They could not tell what complications might arise.

Therefore, not only were Sir Gordon's men instructed to assemble as unobtrusively as possible at all points converging on the quarter itself, but the river, which ran along one part of the noisome place, was selected as the point at which he and Blake would endeavour to break through.

Aside from this secret gathering of his forces, Sir Gordon had decided that they should attempt nothing subtle in the way of a coup. And in this Blake, agreed strongly. It was perfectly obvious that both Wu Ling and the Chuen-to-yan would know that Tinker's disappearance would not be allowed to pass without immediate and strenuous efforts to save the lad. But what Sir Gordon and Blake were counting on was the chance that the two cold-blooded Celestials would believe Blake, and Sir Gordon would not know of the secret slave sale which was planned for that very night. In that lay the only chance of success for Blake.

But in his eyes was that hard, metallic expression which only appeared when Blake was filled with an icy determination for vengeance; and those who knew him well would have guessed that he was bound on some desperate expedition, from which he would return victorious or not at all.

While he was burning inwardly with a terrible anxiety, and, hence, was keenly impatient to get into action, Blake realised perfectly well that to move precipitately was to court failure. Therefore, he revealed no outward sign of what he felt, but, instead, threw himself into the arrangements as if the object of their efforts was simply a pawn in the game they were playing. But he grew calmer as the evening approached, and at the moment when Sir Gordon gave the signal to start, Blake was on his feet like a panther.

Now Sir Gordon had only spoken truth when he said that he had been in the underground burrow known as the Thieves' Market many years before. There were few dens of vice or iniquity in China into which the intriguing and adventurous life of that strange man known as Hsui-fsi had not taken him.

Not even Sexton Blake could have told exactly what deep plotting was even then going on in the brain of that old man who was approaching his ninetieth year. Blake knew a little; and he was content not to try to probe more deeply, for Sir Gordon had been invaluable to him on more than one occasion, and Blake knew that if any living being should be left the legacy of what Hsui-fsi had in his mind, he, Sexton Blake, would be that one.

Moreover, he had implicit confidence in the Oriental cunning which Hsui-fsi had acquired during half a century or more of matching his wits against the most subtle minds of the yellow empire; and, in fact, no other pair except Hsui-fsi and Sexton Blake would have stood the slightest chance against the powerful combination represented by Prince Wu Ling and the ancient Chuen-to-yan.

Before leaving, Sir Gordon posted several men on duty about the garden and in front of the House of Two Hundred Intelligences, for, if things moved along as he hoped, it was a dead certainty that the night would see some strange doings. Nor was he wrong, for the rescue of Tinker was but a part of the plan which the two of them had hammered out that afternoon in the pagoda.

They made their way unobtrusively through the Shameen to the native town, and so on to the river. From time to time a figure would shuffle past close to them and whisper a word in Sir Gordon's ear, which kept them informed of how things were going.

On reaching the river, they stepped into a small, covered sampan, which Blake knew, from numerous rustling sounds, was well filled with men. As a matter of fact, there were more than a score of Hsui-fsi's most trusted adherents concealed inside the sampan; and it is a curious thing that they were there on such a purpose —each one believing that their chief was just, the wise and to be respected Celestial, Hsui-fsi.

Not one conceived for a single moment that beneath that wrinkled and yellow exterior coursed the blood of a pure-bred Englishman. And both Wu Ling and the Chuen-to-yan had their own private reasons for not spreading the fact broadcast.

Not a word was spoken as the sampan was pushed out from the short jetty into the misty river. The man with the steering sweep allowed it to run along on the sluggish current, steering, it seemed, by sheer instinct, through the teeming concourse of other craft which stretched along the river for miles. Now and then they passed close enough to distinguish the vague outlines of another sampan, but, mostly, they were only aware of the teeming life all about them by the sound of voices which reached them through the mist.

It was altogether weird and mysterious and sinister. It was China.

It seemed impossible that the steersman could pilot his craft along through that maze to the spot which was their objective; but, after they had been drifting along for the space of ten minutes or so, Blake was conscious that the man had brought the nose of the sampan round somewhat, and then he began working more vigorously.

They passed under the loftier bows of several junks, then they bumped lightly against what Blake afterwards discovered to be the first of several rows of sampans lining the bank. He found out later, too, that these sampans formed the front line of Sir Gordon's fleet, so to say.

Sir Gordon, despite his years, was the first to step from the sampan on to the nearest one. As easily as the steersman had piloted them through the mist did he lead the little party across line after line of craft, until at last he readied a second short jetty which, Blake could see, jutted out from the rear of a tall, gloomy-looking building. Hsui-fsi crossed the jetty until he reached the wall. He tapped in an odd manner on a part of it, and almost immediately a door swung open. Sir Gordon entered, followed closely by Blake, after whom came the line of Chinese who had been in the sampan.

As the door closed after them they were in complete darkness; but a second later a torch flashed out, and Blake followed Hsui-fsi's example by pressing the switch of his own. He saw that the person who had admitted them was one of the Celestials who had visited Sir Gordon that same afternoon.

It was apparent that no conversation was necessary, for at a sign from Hsui-fsi the man led them through what was nothing more or less than a water-level cellar. It was half filled with a collection of junk of the sort one would pick up along the course of a Chinese river, and the odour was enough to try the nostrils of a bandicoot, and they are not at all particular.

At the back of this cellar their guide busied himself for a few moments with what appeared to be part of the stone wall, and eventually it swung back to reveal a black, gaping hole. Blake knew at once that what he now saw must be one of the hundreds of secret entrances to the underground burrow of the Thieves' Market.

The guide passed through, followed by Sir Gordon, then Blake, and afterwards the line of armed men. But now Blake insisted on passing in front of the old man, for he knew that in a very few minutes they might be in the thick of a melee, and, despite his activity, Sir Gordon was not physically strong enough to stand such a racket.

As if his part of the work had been finished, he gave way without protest, and now it was Blake who moved ahead close at the heels of the guide.

Sexton Blake had been down among the underground passages of old-time Chinatown in San Francisco before the earthquake. He had been through the catacombs of Rome and Paris. He had delved among the ancient secret passages of the old Louvre, and the terrible descending levels of dungeons beneath the old Palais de Justice on the Ile de Cite. He knew pretty well every such system of both ancient and modern times.

But never in his life had he penetrated into such a confusing maze as this beneath the Thieves' Market of Canton. Every few yards they came upon branching passages, which kept increasing the network until it assumed more puzzling proportions than the everglades of Florida or the delta of the Magdalena River.

It was as if they had been reduced by some Eastern magic to the physical proportions of ants, and were moving through some monstrous web which had been drilled through and through in every conceivable direction and at every conceivable angle by those tireless workers. It was a nightmare —sinister, menacing, terrible.

From time to time they passed other figures stealing along through those maddening tunnels; but while some passed without remark, others gave a whispered word to their guide which was sufficient to tell Blake that this section of the underground market, at least, was in the hands of Sir Gordon's men. As they got deeper and deeper into the heart of the place they saw, too, an occasional tallow-flare, or a hanging copper bowl in which a flaming twist of cotton was burning in ground-nut oil.

The passages began to get wider and more lofty, while now the number of other pedestrians increased considerably.

But still it was a place of almost complete silence, broken, only by the shuffle-shuffle of slippered feet and an occasional liquid voice.

It was at a point where half a dozen passages converged that, their guide drew up. He leant back and addressed a few words to Sir Gordon, who then turned to Blake.

"The lad has been brought to the market," he whispered. "The sale is even now taking place. The slave-hall is just along this passage." And he pointed to one on Blake's right. "If we are to take him, it will have to be a quick dash. But we must wait for the main body to break into the slave-hall from above."

"How long will that be?" whispered bark Blake.

"Any moment now they —Ah! They have burst through! No time to lose! Off with you, Blake! Take all the men but two! I will keep this point here for the retreat!"

Blake needed no second bidding. With a sign to the men behind him, he drew out a heavy automatic and started running along the passage which led to what Sir Gordon had called the "slave-hall." It was no great distance, for Blake could distinctly hear the sounds of a growing tempest of shrill yells, and in less than a hundred yards he burst upon the scene.

He saw before him a large, circular apartment which had been hollowed out of the bowels of the earth. A rude attempt had been made to line the walk with slabs of stone, while the floor was covered with dirty matting, and the ceiling had been plastered over with a yellowish white substance.

From the ceiling hung half a dozen copper ground-nut oil lamps, which gave a flickering illumination to the place, and at one end was a rude platform, on which Blake could now see several figures and about which the main struggle seemed to be centering.

Blake paused for a moment until he made out a figure standing bound in the very centre of the stage. Even at the distance and through the smoke of the place the white skin marked him as different from those who were shrieking and howling about him. He was naked to the waist. His hands seemed to have been bound, and across his chest were streaks of crimson which caused Blake to curse sharply as he saw them.

But even in that den of vileness, in the face of what had seemed certain slavery and torture, in the teeth of that shrieking mob of Celestials, under the myriad flashes of those sweeping, crimsoning blades, the lad stood with head proudly uplifted and eyes gazing upon the yellow ranks with cool contempt.

They had tortured his body, but they had not even bent his spirit.

All this Blake took in in a single glance. Then, with a harsh command in the dialect, he dashed forward, shooting as he went. He was glad that the Celestials were using knives only, for the automatic undoubtedly gave him an advantage which, backed by the eighteen who were following him close, and who were also armed with revolvers, made their arrival a big asset to those of Sir Gordon's men who had already succeeded in bursting into the place.

But Blake knew that scores and scores of reinforcements would soon arrive, and if Tinker were to be saved, it would have to be quick.

He was shooting with cold calculation as he ran, and as Tinker turned his head in the direction of the sound of shots, Blake knew that he had recognised him. He could see the lad straining madly at his bonds for an instant, but then the yellow flood swept over him and he became lost to view.

Blake reached the outer line of the struggling mass just as an upheaval in the centre caused it to break slightly. He fired point-blank at a man who was in the act of hurling his knife at him; then, pushed on by his own men, he forced a way through until he was less than a dozen feet from the platform.

A second sudden upheaval of the mob threw Blake back again, but as he saw half a dozen hands reaching out as if to drag Tinker into some place of safety from rescue he felt the strength of two men course through him. He hurled himself against that living wall like a madman, and by sheer fury drove a path through.

Man after man he sent down until he had cut him a path to the very edge of the platform.

Somehow he managed to get up on it.

Miraculously, it seemed, his men stemmed the press while he jerked out a knife and slit Tinker's bonds.

A hurried word between them, then Blake turned to fight a way back.

But in the melee his queue had fallen loose, and his wig had been jerked off.

So furiously had he been fighting that Blake had not noticed it. Nor had any of the others until just then, as they saw him turn.

At the sight a shrill squeal went up, and as Blake jumped down off the platform, handing Tinker a spare weapon, the mob concentrated on trying to reach them.

It seemed hopeless that they could ever cut a way through that press of yellow devils. In fact, it would have been an impossibility unless the wise old Hsui-fsi had not put in an appearance at that critical moment with reinforcements recruited from his sampans on the river. As half a hundred men poured into the place the press broke a little, and before the deadly bullets of the automatics gave way.

Blake seized his chance.

He was subconsciously aware that they were through, that they were surrounded by Sir Gordon's men, that they were dashing wildly through a maze of damp, evil-smelling passages, and then that somehow they were tumbling over line after line of sampans until they fell headlong into a cabin.

A moment later the silent, imperturbable steersman had pushed the sampan out into the mist, and the three Europeans sat up, panting, worn, wounded and battered, but victorious.

It seemed hopeless that they could ever cut a way through that press of yellow devils. In fact, it would have been an impossibility had not old Hsui-fsi opportunely appeared with his reinforcements, recruited from the sampans of the river. (*Chapter* 6.)

Wu Ling himself confronted Tinker. But the lad, helpless as he was, told him that he and his yellow fiends could kill him before he would speak. Moreover, Wu Ling saw that he meant it. (*Chapter* 7.)

AS soon as they were clear Blake questioned Tinker anxiously as to his condition, slipping his own coat round him to cover his scarred torso.

"They gave me a bad time of it, guv'nor," responded the lad, in a tone of weariness, "but I am all right. They put me under the lash this afternoon in order to try and make me tell what I knew of you and Hsui-fsi. But they didn't get anything out of me; only I hope I live long enough to ferret out the chief sacrificial priest of the Temple of Internal Light."

Blake gritted his teeth.

"Was that where they lashed you?" he asked, in an ominous tone.

"Yes. I'll tell you how it happened, guv'nor. When Wu Ling turned up I followed him into the small temple. By luck and some strategy I managed to discover the secret passage that leads from that temple to the other. I followed it along, and, after a considerable time, had reached what I knew must be the other temple. But just as I turned a corner of the passage I ran full tilt into a giant.

"He must have been close to seven feet, and you can take it from me he was the ugliest human I have ever seen. I found out later he was the head sacrificial priest of the place,"

"I have seen him once," said Blake; while Sir Gordon muttered something to himself in the dark which neither of them could catch. "Go on!"

"He choked me into insensibility, and I didn't know any more until I came to, to find myself lying on the floor of a huge underground apartment. Before me, on a kind of throne, was seated an old, old man dressed all in white.

"I knew soon that he was the Chuen-to-yan. Seated near him was Wu Ling. They were discussing me, and when Wu Ling saw I was conscious he began to question me. Of course, I refused to answer, so, a little later, the Chuen-to-yan gave an order.

"The sacrificial priest, with about twenty armed men, carried me into a small stone chamber, where they strapped me to a stone post. Then —well then, they just began to leather me properly. Wu Ling came in while it was going on, and again questioned me. I told him they could kill me before they would make me speak, and I guess he saw I meant it, for I did.

"He told them to let up then, and informed me that I would go to a worse fate. Of course, I knew pretty well what he meant, but I knew all the time that you would be doing everything in your power to reach me. Well, this evening they dragged me along to that place where you saw me, and that's all."

"And enough!" snarled Blake. "As soon as we reach the House of Two Hundred Intelligences you are going to bed, my lad, and have your wounds treated. As for the sacrificial priest, let your mind rest easy. I give you my word that you will be avenged before we leave Canton."

And Tinker was too nearly all in to argue the point.

They made their way back to Sir Gordon's house the way they had come. No one attempted to molest them, but on the way Sir Gordon received several swiftly whispered reports, which appeared to give him considerable satisfaction.

They were to the effect that his men had made a sanguinary clean up at the Thieves' Market, and had managed to get away before any large number of reinforcements arrived from either Wu Ling or the Chuen-to-yan.

As a matter of fact, of the many frequent and gory tong battles which take place in the native part of Canton, the affair that night was destined to rank as one of the most terrible, and it says a good deal for the system controlled by Hsui-fsi that he was able to bring off such a coup at a time when not only were Wu Ling and the Chuen-to-yan both in Canton, but were also leagued together against him.

As for what passed as the Government, not one of the factions gave the matter a single thought. They knew that as long as the struggle was kept out of the Shameen nothing would be said or done.

On reaching the House of Two Hundred Intelligences, Blake and Sir Gordon made an examination of Tinker's wounds. The skin was torn badly in more than a score of places, and across his back there ran great ugly welts where the lash had caught him. Blake ground his teeth in rage as he gently bathed them, and renewed silently the threat of vengeance he had uttered in the sampan.

His chance was to come sooner than he thought.

While Blake completed the work of attending to the lad and getting him into bed, Sir Gordon departed on some mysterious mission, the purport of which only Blake knew. And knowing this, Blake realised that yet was to come the real test of strength between him and Hsui-fsi, as opposed to Wu Ling and Chuen-to-yan.

On the way back to the house Sir Gordon had been informed, among other things, that Wu Ling had again visited the Temple of Eternal Light that evening, and was, it appeared, closeted with the Chuen-to-yan. This caused Blake and the old man to opine that final conditions were being discussed between the two arch-plotters, and they knew if ever the combination was to be smashed it must be that very night.

But this was a time when brute force would not serve. The affair at the Thieves' Market had been sufficient to put the enemy on guard against any repetition of such a daring coup.

Only subtle finesse would serve, and while Sir Gordon had put forward a plan, which was as full of simple guile as even the Chuen-to-yan could have mustered, it depended for its success on certain given conditions. And they could not possibly know if these conditions would obtain until at the very moment when the plan must be tried.

In other words, they could not tell until they were on the ground whether they stood a chance or not, and since that ground was the underground apartment of the Chuen-to-yan, it can be understood just how daring was their scheme, for they two —and they two alone — stood any chance of entering that den of mystery and intrigue. That they would be admitted, they knew, for Sir Gordon —or, rather, Hsui-fsi had as much right of ingress there, through his powerful connections, as did Wu Ling.

Nor did they anticipate that any attempt to assassinate them would be made, for, after the fashion of the European churches of the Middle Ages, the Temple of Eternal Light was a place of sanctuary which even the Chuen-to-yan would not violate. The ancient priest might scheme and plot for temporal power in China, as well as religious power; but, withal, he was a devout Buddhist, and, even if he were not, he would not dare, as supreme head of the Buddhist faith in China, to violate one of the most stringent laws laid down by the Buddha.

Now, in order to understand the exact position of this underground apartment of the Chuen-to-yan, and how it was Hsui-fsi hit upon the subtle plan which he proposed to Blake, and which Blake elaborated, it is necessary to explain that the Temple of Eternal Light —as, indeed, was the Temple of Ancient Virtues and other temples of

China —was almost as extensive underground as it was above ground.

Probably no really modern buildings have to any extent equalled this idea in architecture until the creation of the modern skyscrapers in New York and other American cities.

But the same idea was followed in Europe during the Middle Ages, and thus we find that, in the case of the Louvre, for example, of noble Notre Dame de Paris, of the now demolished Bastille, and even the old Palais de Justice in Paris, there were several layers of cells and dungeons below the ground level, it being said in the case of the older part of the Louvre that some of these foul holes descended fully two hundred feet below the level of the Seine, and that from the very deepest, where many dark and awful crimes took place, there were secret passages leading to the river.

In such a way, untold centuries ago, had the Temple of Eternal Light been built. Only the hereditary Chuen-to-yan knew just how far down they extended, but it is certain that even worse tortures and crimes than ever were perpetrated by a Medici, a Borgia, or even the ferocious and blood-lustful old Empress Dowager, in the hidden city in Pekin, had taken place in those deeps.

How true it was that the present Chuen-to-yan had ruled as supreme head of the Buddhist faith in China for a hundred and fifty years, the writer is not prepared to say; but certainly Sir Gordon Saddler assured Sexton Blake that he, personally, had seen religious edicts dated fully that long ago, and signed by him who was to-day the Chuen-to-yan.

It may seem incredible to us of the West, but it is a fact that there still lives in Turkey a man whose age is reliably computed to be a hundred and forty-four, and who actually journeyed to Paris last year. And it is difficult to estimate just how long a strict ascetic, who has reached the stage of an adept, and who follows the strictest spiritual, mental, and physical regime, might live.

The apartment in which the Chuen-to-yan remained as a greater recluse than any Pope was the second below the level of the ground. It was a vast hall surrounded by several small chambers, into which, only the Chuen-to-yan was allowed to enter, apart from the deaf mutes who served him, and, who were scarcely human beings, it is said there were three hundred and sixty-five pillars holding up the lofty-domed ceiling, the upper ends of which were lost in the eternal gloom above.

These pillars, like those on a smaller scale in the Temple of Ancient Virtues, were covered by the most minute and intricate of mosaics and arabesques, revealing every possible tone of colour, but yet all subordinate to the sacred and royal saffron.

The floor was a masterpiece of marble tiling, set off in strange figures and patterns, which were really taken from incidents in the life of Buddha. The walls were covered with wonderfully carved scenes in relief, which were a full history of the whole life of Buddha, and which, from their Hindu characteristics, were proof that they had been cut there many centuries ago, when the religion was first brought as a mild philosophic faith from India, and before it had degenerated into the fantastic and cruel creed which the twisted Chinese mind had made of it.

Between the pillars were hung gorgeously coloured silken banners, bearing strange devices, while at one end —the throne end —was a raised dais of black marble, covered with a rich Eastern rug, and on which was a carved throne of ivory and gold, which would have suffered not at all by comparison with the famous peacock throne of the Grand Mogul.

Above this throne were more silken banners, bearing the private cipher of the Chuen-to-yan, hanging from wide frames of pure gold. And flanking the throne on either side were statues of the goddess of light and the goddess of virtue, as interpreted by the Celestial, and which, needless to say, were very different from what would have been interpreted by a Western artist.

And, above all, was a marvellous gold inlaid statue of the great Dhabutsa himself, towering fully thirty feet above the throne, where two giant sapphires of unrivalled size and purity had been placed in the eye sockets. No throne-room of any age in history was more wondrously beautiful than that apartment of the Chuen-to-yan of the Temple of Eternal Light.

And it was into this secret and sacred apartment that Hsui-fsi and Sexton Blake were conducted after they had entered the ground hall of the temple.

On attempting to descend their passage had been barred by the gigantic and hideous chief sacrificial priest, at sight of whom Blake bad as much as he could do to keep his fingers off the automatic which he had placed in the pocket of the wide, loose sleeve of the embroidered tunic which he wore. But recollection of a certain thing Sir Gordon carried in the pocket of the sleeve of his tunic served to make him stay his hand. It was not the time then to exact payment for the indignity which had been put upon Tinker.

At a few words and a sign from Sir Gordon the priest was forced to yield the way, and, at a sort of growl which he emitted, two of the Chuen-to-yan's soldiers, armed with pikes like soldiers of the Middle Ages, stepped out of the gloom to form an escort. Sir Gordon and Blake followed them at once, but both of them saw fully a score more soldiers step in behind them and form a rearguard.

Under flickering torches of ground-nut oil they passed along several stonewalled passages, and then down a winding, narrow staircase, on which Blake counted a hundred steps before they reached the bottom, and which, at each of its dozen or more landings, was guarded by a soldier armed to the teeth.

Then along another passage, past a close-drawn guard of half a dozen more soldiers, and then suddenly into the vast hall of the private audience chamber of the Chuen-to-yan. They advanced side by side until they were half up the hall, when only then were they able to distinguish the wizened, white-clad figure who was seated on the ancient throne of the Chuen-to-yans of China.

And the next instant Blake's keen gaze made out another figure seated on the ground level, but close to the edge of the dais. It was Prince Wu Ling, garbed in the richest ceremonial robes which, as of the Manchu blood royal, and supreme head of the Brotherhood of the Yellow Beetle, he was privileged to wear.

AS they approached nearer, and finally came to a stop just half a dozen feet from the throne, Blake could make out distinctly the multitude of wrinkles that criss-crossed the shrunken countenance of the Chuen-to-yan in the most extraordinary fashion. If it hadn't taken a hundred and fifty years or more to accomplish that, it had taken not far from it.

Yet the yellow, parchment-like skin was a fit setting for the deep-set, oblique eyes which glared out like two hard, black marbles from beneath a brow that was utterly devoid of hair. The whole pate was absolutely guiltless of anything even faintly approaching the hirsute, and the skull looked extraordinarily big and wide under the tight-drawn skin, which seemed infinitely more smooth and part of the very skull than that of Sir Gordon, though Blake had thought that no pate could be barer than that of Hsui-fsi.

The nose was not broad and wide-nostrilled like that of the ordinary Chinese. It was arched and high, with high-cut, cruel nostrils, and a mouth that was lipless. The chin was sharp, pointed, and long —the chin of a human beast of prey. The figure was tiny, and shrunken to an amazing degree, but which was natural enough in an adept. He was clothed in rich robes of white silk, which were swathed about and about him, as if he were a mummy.

Altogether, it was a most extraordinary being upon whom Blake looked, but one, he knew, of infinite wisdom and infinite capacity for cruelty. In those black, hard eyes there seemed to float the very essence of all the evil which had passed since man had first drunk from the bottomless cup of sin.

For some minutes none of that strange quartette uttered a word. The two who stood were gazing impassively at the Chuen-to-yan, while the latter had his eyes fixed on Hsui-fsi. Wu Ling was regarding Blake under lowered lids. It was the Chuen-to-yan, who first broke the heavy silence.

"What seek you here, Hsui-fsi?" he asked abruptly, in harsh, unaccented English, and making no attempt to utter any of the usual flowery phrases of the East.

Sir Gordon's face crinkled into a smile. He did not reply at once, but raising his arm, pointed towards a slim, black marble shaft about five feet high, and on the top of which could just be discerned a tiny object. Blake's eyes followed the direction of the arm, and something gave a jump inside him as he recognised the Ling-tse vase.

So there was proof that Hsui-fsi had been right!

Chan had been a servant of the Chuen-to-yan, and had succeeded in reaching Canton with the vase. That meant their second theory — that Wu Ling was trying to arrange a working alliance with the Chuen-to-yan —was right, too.

"Chan has served you well," said Sir Gordon slowly, as he lowered his arm. "You ask what we seek here, O pious Chuen-to-yan. I will tell you. It is said that the sacred Ling-tse vase has been copied. Like his Excellency, Prince Wu Ling, we have a desire to know if that vase which rests near you is the true Ling-tse vase, or the copy which was made. There have been other copies, too, as his Excellency, the prince, knows full well, and somewhat to his chagrin."

"If that is what you seek you need exercise your mind no longer," responded the Chuen-to-yan dryly. "You and the accursed foreign devil who is with you, and who chooses to go clad as a mandarin of the purple button, are protected by the law of sanctuary in coming here; but beware, Hsui-fsi! If you have some mad plan for getting possession of the sacred Ling-tse vase, abandon it while you have time. I, Chuen-to-yan of the Temple of Eternal Light, tell you that this vase which you see; is the only true and sacred vase, which all true Buddhists must reverence as sacred. Seek not to commit sacrilege!"

Hsui-fsi bowed.

"The Chuen-to-yan speaks, and I hear." he said, in slow, almost gentle, tones. "The Chuen-to-yan knows that neither I, nor my friend who is with me, would be so mad as to try to tear the vase from where it rests, and take it from the temple. Sanctuary does not cover the sacred vase, whose true altar is in the north and not here in the south, but well we know that, did we attempt to take it in such fashion, we would be killed the moment we passed over the threshold of the temple.

"Yet I would satisfy myself, by mine own eyes, that it is indeed the sacred and true vase. Surely the Chuen-to-yan, who has the assistance of his Excellency, Prince Wu Ling, who is in his own stronghold, surrounded by his own soldiers, has no doubt of his own power?"

And the old man's tones took on a mocking timbre, as he smiled again.

The Chuen-to-yan regarded him in silence for what seemed to Blake a very long time. It was perfectly plain that the Chuen-to-yan suspected Hsui-fsi of trying to trick him in some way, but it didn't seem possible that he and Blake unsupported could bring off anything there in his own stronghold, where, as Hsui-fsi had said, he was guarded by his own soldiers.

And yet he knew Hsui-fsi of old —he knew the capacity for cunning which the mystery man possessed, and he knew he would need his acutest wits to match it.

Perhaps he would even then have played for safety by refusing the request had not Wu Ling uttered a single remark full of contempt for Hsui-fsi and Blake. It was this which apparently decided the Chuen-to-yan, who, despite his recent alliance with Wu Ling, had no love for the northern prince.

Without speaking, he reached out, and, with infinite care, took

56

down the tiny vase about which such terrible passions had raged through the centuries. He held it carefully; then, looking at Hsui-fsi, he said:

"You may satisfy yourself that this is the true vase on two conditions."

"They are?"

"You must give me your word of honour that neither you nor the one who is with you will in any way attempt to damage it."

"I give that gladly. The vase is as precious to me as to you. The second?"

"That neither you nor the one who is with you will make any attempt to take the vase from this temple."

"I pledge you my word that neither of us will attempt to take the vase away with us."

"You answer for the other?"

"Yes."

"Then take it."

With that the Chuen-to-yan held out the vase, which Hsui-fsi took cautiously. As his fingers closed about it, he stepped back a few paces until he was directly under one of the flambeaux. There he bent his head over it, while Blake drew close also, under pretence of examining it. As for the Chuen-to-yan and Wu Ling, they were watching the pair like a couple of cobras ready to strike. And well they might, for now the critical moment had been reached.

If that pair of cunning Celestials was to be outwitted, it must be now or never.

While they bent over it, Sir Gordon nodded his head slowly a few times, as if to confirm the fact that it was indeed the true vase. But, under cover of one of these motions, he whispered the single word "Now!" to Blake.

At that things began to happen.

Sexton Blake stiffened, while Sir Gordon swung round with a speed extraordinary in one of his age. The next second his right hand had shot into the loose pocket of the left sleeve of his tunic, and, as if the effect had been produced by a conjurer, something dark appeared, fluttering in his hand. For one tense moment Sir Gordon's hand hovered close to the object, and then, just as the Chuen-to-yan and Wu Ling gave an inarticulate cry, a blue homing pigeon rose in bewildered fashion above their heads. It was still hovering uncertainly, confused by the smoke of the flambeaux, when, with a mad growl of rage, the chief sacrificial priest, who had been standing in the shadow of one of the pillars, sprang forward, his spear poised ready to hurl into the breast of Hsui-fsi.

For the moment all law of sanctuary had been forgotten, but, even as the spear was loosed, Sexton Blake's hand came up.

In it was a heavy automatic. There was a crack; the bullet caught the sacrificial priest full between the eyes, and he went down with a dull thud. The spear ripped through the silk of Sir Gordon's tunic, but the old man was only staggered by the blow.

He did not even lower his eyes as he reached up mechanically and drew out the shaft.

His gaze was fixed on the tiny, hardly discernible speck which was flashing back and forth in the gloom high above. Beyond holding up his hand to sign his soldiers to stand back, the Chuen-to-yan took no further notice of the incident which had so nearly cost Sir Gordon his life, and which had forced Blake to violate the law of sanctuary of the temple.

His gaze, too, was fixed on the pigeon, while Wu Ling sat, head uplifted in a way that reminded Blake of a hawk.

Never had any of that four passed through a more tense strain than they endured during the next few minutes. High above them was the homing pigeon, bearing the sacred and priceless Ling-tse vase in a specially prepared little padded bag which had been fixed to its leg. It had taken Blake and Sir Gordon a full hour to adjust that bag to their liking.

If the bird failed to find an opening, the coup had missed fire, and, not only that, but in its wild dashes the pigeon might bring disaster to the vase. It was a moment when the fate of four hundred millions of human beings hung by a frail thread. And still back and forth the pigeon flew, seeking valiantly for an exit.

There was what it sought all right, and Sir Gordon knew where it was —a cunningly contrived ventilation tunnel leading to an opening under the eaves of the topmost roof of the temple. It was that which he and Blake were praying the pigeon would find —that its instinct and some faint current of air would guide it. And the two gave a sharp exclamation of relief as suddenly the pigeon darted away through the gloom, to return no more.

It had found the opening.

Blake lowered his gaze and turned towards the Chuen-to-yan. That shrunken countenance was as devoid of expression as ever, but as he gazed upon those hard, black eyes, Blake felt rather than saw a something which, despite the iron control of the adept, had forced itself out from the terrible rage which was twisting the spirit inside.

He turned still more to regard Wu Ling. The prince had found it impossible to match the sublime control of the Chuen-to-yan. His eyes were fixed on Hsui-fsi with an expression which Sexton Blake had seen there once before, and which he read aright.

It boded no good for either of them once Wu Ling should find a weapon of offence.

Then his eyes fell on Hsui-fsi, and, for all the acute tension of their position, Blake could not help allowing a faint reflection of an inward smile creep into his eyes, for Hsui-fsi was standing gazing at the discomfited pair of arch plotters, a hand in either loose sleeve, his wrinkled countenance screwed up in a most alarming manner.

He was laughing, laughing soundlessly, with an unholy enjoyment of the situation which would have done credit to the Chuen-to-yan himself; and, still again, Blake found it almost incredible of belief that this old man, who could so successfully match his cunning and guile against the East, could be of pure British blood.

And it was while he was still convulsed by that soundless mirth that Sir Gordon took Blake's arm and led the way along between the giant pillars towards the passage by which they would reach the street. Blake took one look at the crumpled form of the sacrificial priest, who had paid in full for the indignity and suffering he had inflicted upon Tinker, then he gazed straight ahead towards the opening which meant freedom and victory.

And, although the guards shifted uneasily, neither the Chuen-to-yan nor Wu Ling said them nay.

THE END.
[23500 WORDS]

The chief priest sprang forward, his spear poised to hurl into the breast of Hsui-fsi. But, even as the spear was loosed, Blake's hand came up. There was a crack, and the sacrificial priest fell backwards. The spear ripped through the silk of Sir Gordon's tunic. (*Chapter 8.*)

TINKER - MOTOR-CYCLIST!

Next Thursday's yarn is a thriller. It is written round that most exciting of motor cycle road-races, the Senior Tourist Trophy contest, which is fought out in the Isle of Man next week.

The plot is ingenious, the action swift, and the climax breathlessly thrilling. Motorcyclist or not, you will infallibly enjoy this grand story —a topical tale of TINKER'S TOURIST TROPHY.

Watch for the arresting blue-and-yellow cover. And, in the meantime, order your copy, and make certain of not being disappointed.

THE UNION JACK 2ᴰ

THE CASE OF
TINKER'S
TOURIST
TROPHY

An Exciting Yarn of Detective Work and Motor Racing
Full of thrills, and Complete in this issue.
Introducing SEXTON BLAKE and TINKER.

No. 1,027.   EVERY THURSDAY   June 10th, 1923.

62

In response to many enquiries, some more stories of various old favourites are being arranged for, including the Confederation and Waldo the Wonder-man. The creator of the latter character is in California, where he is gathering "local colour" for some yarns written round this popular character. The stories that result will be published as early as possible. Look out for future announcements.

THE SUPPLEMENT.

Our forthcoming programme for the D.M.S. is a very attractive one. It includes:

THE EXTREME PENALTY. —All about the methods of execution in various countries.

PUNISHMENTS OF THE PAST —Old-time ways of enforcing the law by means of mechanical devices such as the **Scold's Bridle**, etc.

TYBURN TREE. —An account of the famous gallows of historic London.

DYNAMITERS' DASTARDLY DEEDS. —Some of the explosion plots that have resounded throughout the world.

IN THE CONDEMNED CELL OF OLD NEWGATE, etc., etc.

SCOLD'S BRIDLE
-
THE
HORRIFIC
PUNISHMENT
FOR
"DIFFICULT
WOMEN"

CHINESE MARKET SACRAMENTO ST.

Printed and published every Thursday by the Proprietors, The Amalgamated Press (1922). Ltd., The Fleetway House, Farringdon Street, London, E.O.4. Advertisement offices: The Fleetway House, Farringdon Street, London, E.0.4 Subscription rates: Inland and Abroad, 11s. per annum; 5s. 6d. for six months. Sole agents for South Africa: The Central News Agency, Ltd. Sole agents for Australia and New Zealand: Messrs. Gordon & Gotch, Ltd.; and for Canada, The Imperial News Co., Ltd. (Canada).— Saturday, June 9th, 1923.

My copy of this story/issue has only 17 of at least 26 pages. /drf

www.ingramcontent.com/pod-product-compliance
Lightning Source LLC
Chambersburg PA
CBHW050904120626
46554CB00003B/1012